IT TOO[K]
LESS T[HAN] [T]HIRTY SECONDS

to strip the stock from the Sten and attach one of the thirty-two-round magazines. He then slid the gun up under his blouse and used the stock clips to secure it to the ties around his chest.

Carter checked and then rechecked his arms. When he was completely satisfied that he could get to everything in a split second, he hoisted a roll of netting to his left shoulder and set off.

Without altering his pace, the Killmaster closed his fingers over the butt of Wilhelmina.

The moon chose that moment—when he was about forty yards from the junk's bow—to come out full, bathing him in a cold, white light. . . .

NICK CARTER IS IT!

FROM THE NICK CARTER
KILLMASTER SERIES

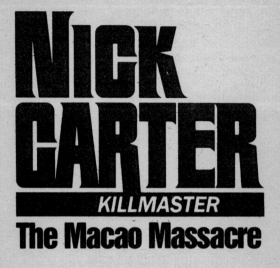

NICK CARTER

KILLMASTER

The Macao Massacre

CHARTER BOOKS, NEW YORK

THE MACAO MASSACRE

A Charter Book/published by arrangement with
The Condé Nast Publications, Inc.

PRINTING HISTORY
Charter Original/March 1985

ISBN: 0-441-51353-0

Charter Books are published by The Berkley Publishing Group,
200 Madison Avenue, New York, New York 10016.
PRINTED IN THE UNITED STATES OF AMERICA

Dedicated to the men of the
Secret Services of the
United States of America

The Macao Massacre

ONE

Nick Carter awoke to the aroma of freshly brewed coffee. He stretched, then allowed a wide grin to spread across his face as he patted the vacant spot beside him on the bed and remembered the previous evening.

Her name was Fancy Adams, and she was everything her name implied. She was a free-lancer, outside AXE, but very trustworthy and often used for low-key work.

She and Carter had teamed up on a couple of assignments in years past, but this time it was only a lucky, chance meeting.

Very lucky, for Carter.

Fancy had been on assignment in Tokyo, doing public relations work and some commercials for an American cosmetics company launching a new line in the Far East.

At least that was her cover. Actually, she was doing a piece of surveillance among a big group of powerful Japanese businessmen for the CIA boys. Now she had been called back to Washington for a debriefing.

Carter didn't know what the assignment was, and he didn't care. What he did care about was running into her at Pavels, a bistro off the Washington Beltway that he frequented when he was between assignments himself.

"My God, Fancy Adams! It's been . . . two years!"

"I agree, two years too long," she said with a laugh, folding into his arms. "Miami, right?"

"Right."

It had been Miami. Fancy had been a pawn in a plan that enabled Carter to disappear and get a defector from the Eastern bloc into Spain to find a little black book hidden behind an ebony cross.

Before they had parted, he and Fancy had spent a wild two days in a Miami hotel room.

Carter hadn't forgotten it.

He asked if she had.

"Are you kidding?" she said, her green eyes flashing under a mountain of red hair.

"Who are you with?"

"Some of the guys from the Company. Strictly platonic."

She went on to explain where she had been for the last month, and what she was doing in Washington.

"Where are you staying?"

"A Company condo here in Arlington."

"What would happen if you didn't make it home tonight?" Carter asked mischievously.

"Not a damned thing," she replied and smiled. "I'm debriefed, and I head back to New York day after tomorrow."

"Then why don't we check you out of your condo tonight, and for the next two days—"

"Say no more!"

She said good night to her three escorts, and two hours later they were romping on the king-size bed in Carter's own condominium apartment on the top floor of an Arlington highrise.

And what a romp it had been, Carter thought, breathing deeply of the aromas wafting from his kitchen. With a full day and a night to go!

He rolled from the bed and slipped into a robe.

He entered the kitchen, and Fancy popped into view from behind the refrigerator door. Her fiery curls were still disheveled, a pretty mass of red framing her fine features and flashing green eyes. Right now, those eyes were gleaming with cheerful good spirits.

"You're up," she grinned, blowing him a kiss.

She was wearing a deep green silk kimono, haphazardly belted, and the sunlight through the kitchen windows made the bare flesh of her legs and belly and breasts gleam enticingly.

"Good morning," Carter said, slipping his arms around her waist and kissing the soft hollow of her neck.

"It is now," she murmured.

She laughed softly as his hands moved down over the smooth swell of her buttocks.

Carter groaned, and she leaned harder against him in response. Her shapely bottom was firm and round beneath the silk.

"Breakfast is ready. Just orange juice, coffee, and toast. I was just getting the juice." As she spoke, she parted her thighs and captured one of his between them.

Carter chuckled and pulled back. "I'll get it," he said, moving to the refrigerator, "or the coffee will be cold by the time we get to it."

"Something wrong?" Fancy asked coyly, knowing full well how she was affecting him.

He carried the plastic decanter to the drop-leaf table and concentrated on filling the two glasses already set out beside the coffee mugs. "No, nothing . . . nothing at all. How was Tokyo?"

Fancy slid into the breakfast nook beside him, thigh to thigh, and began jabbering about the trials and tribulations of being a model at a foreign show.

Carter sipped his coffee and watched her over the rim of the mug. He was enjoying the sound of her voice almost as much as the sight of her partially concealed nudity. It never ceased to amaze him how she could be so totally unaffected and uninhibited by the lack of clothing, and how she was often surprised to find that her indifference was capable of embarrassing and arousing him.

He found himself looking at her large and beautifully rounded breasts. They swayed weightily with each gesture of her hands, and he watched in fascination, remembering the feel of them and the taste of them and the delight of them.

She laughed throatily. "I wish you'd stop staring at me that way, Nick. It's very disconcerting."

"Come here," he whispered, pulling at her hand and guiding her around the table to his lap. He kissed the freely offered lips and filled his hand with her breast, his thumb gently and lovingly massaging the blunted tip. Fancy breathed into his mouth and caressed his lips with her tongue, her fingertips toying with his ear. "You like to be touched, don't you?" Carter murmured, feeling the nipple begin to harden.

"I love it," she answered softly, leaning back into him.

"I know a better place to do the touching."

He picked her up and headed for the bedroom. Halfway to the bed, the phone started ringing.

"Forget it," Fancy said, clawing at his shoulders when he turned from her.

"Can't. It's the hot one."

There were two phone lines into Carter's apartment. One was a regular line. The other was on a scrambler and connected directly to the office of AXE's number one man, David Hawk.

"Yeah, Carter here."

"It's Ginger, Nick."

"Damn."

Ginger Bateman was Hawk's right hand, his alter ego, and the one who usually relayed Hawk's orders to move. She hardly ever called him unless something was hot.

"It's not as bad as you may think," Ginger said with a chuckle.

"I'll bet," Carter replied, shifting his eyes to Fancy Adams. She had removed the kimono and was now sprawled across the bed with her legs invitingly open.

"There's a gentleman in the San Francisco area very anxious to get in touch with you."

"I don't know anybody in San Francisco anymore," Carter said. "They're all dead."

"This one is very much alive, and the reason I'm passing it on is that he knows most of the right numbers to call to get in touch with you. I think you'll agree that's pretty unusual."

Carter's antennae went up, and for the moment he forgot about Fancy Adams's luscious body. AXE was probably the U.S. government's most secret organization. As the top agent of AXE, with an N3 Killmaster designation, Nicholas Carter was just as supersecret.

If somebody knew enough to try and reach him at Amalgamated Press and Wire Services on Dupont Circle in Washington, D.C., that somebody was either an old friend or an old foe.

In either case, Carter was interested.

"What's the name?"

"Wouldn't give one," Ginger replied. "He sounded Oriental, and like it was an emergency. He's called three times since I got into the office at seven this morning. Since that's four in the morning West Coast time, he must really want to get in touch with you."

"Did he say what it's about?"

"Not a word. But the last time he called, he said you would remember him from Operation Crossroads."

Carter did a quick flip of his mental file and came up with the bare bones of Operation Crossroads.

It was in the thick of the Vietnam mess. He had been sent in undercover to Saigon as an auditor for army supply. His real job had been to uncover a huge black market ring.

Using blackmail, a top-dog smuggler named Charlie Loo had put together a combine of South Vietnamese generals.

The generals gave Charlie Loo free rein on incoming war

supplies in return for his silence about their own nefarious affairs. Loo used his influence to steal the army blind. In turn, he bought dope with the proceeds. A lot of it he exported, but he also sold a ton of it to American GIs.

Carter was able to break up the ring, but he never nailed Charlie Loo.

Ginger Bateman was speaking again. "Well, ring any bells?"

"Several."

"He gave me a number, 555-4027. I've already checked it out. It's a Chinese restaurant in Marin County called Lu Fong's Hunan House."

"I'll buzz him," Carter said.

"Have a nice day."

"Thanks. *Ciao*."

Carter killed the connection, waited for the tone, and dialed.

It was answered on the first ring.

"Yeah?"

"My name is Carter."

"If it is, you can probably tell me where to get the best piece of ass in Saigon."

"Mama Puang's in Cherry Hills."

"How right you are. What do you like to drink?"

"Three fingers of Chivas with one cube."

"Christ, Nick, am I glad I got a hold of you!"

Carter had been grappling with the voice. Suddenly he had it.

"Billy Duong?"

"In the flesh, my man!"

Carter smiled as he remembered the little man with the wide, toothy smile, the flashing black eyes, and the brilliant mind.

Billy Duong had been one of two people who had helped Carter knock Charlie Loo out of the saddle. The other had been a beautiful Eurasian lady from the States.

She was dead, compliments of Charlie Loo.

"What the hell are you doing in the States?"

"Long story, Nick, very long story. But I'm sure glad I learned GI English. It's a great cover."

"Cover? Cover for what?"

"I'm in up to my ass, Nick. And guess how I got that way? . . . By going straight, would you believe!"

"What's up?"

"Too long for the phone. Can you fly out here right away, today?"

"Maybe. Lay a little of it on me so I can give my people an excuse for expenses."

"Okay, but quick. After the old homeland went belly-up, I knocked around for about three years, mostly Hong Kong. My sister's still there. Then I got me some legit papers, and with those, a legit job with Kulo Electronics. It's a Japanese outfit."

"I know it."

"Well, being the genius I am, I go up in the company. They bring me to the home office in Tokyo about a year ago. About three months ago, I get hassled by three very bad dudes."

"Billy, if you were shifting funds or something, that's out of—"

"No way, Nick. I'm strictly legit, loyal, and faithful. But as you know, my past is not lily-white."

"To say the least," Carter agreed with a chuckle.

"Laugh you might, but these dudes know all about me and my past. I'm in the company under the name of William Soo Luong, with a phony degree from Stanford and MIT in the States."

"That figures," Carter groaned.

"Yeah, well, they want me to steal blueprints and specs and hand them over to them, or they expose me."

"Old-fashioned blackmail?"

"You got it. Well, ole Billy is pissed. I figure I can be as shifty as they are. I do some digging, and come up with a lot.''

"Like who's behind it?"

"Yeah, like Charlie Loo."

The hair stood up and the skin rippled on the back of Carter's neck.

"You still there?"

"Yeah," Carter said, "I'm still here. Tell me more."

"Charlie's got his old scam going, full blast, right there in Japan. When I get enough, I figure this is bigger than my pride or my job. I dump it all in my big boss's lap.''

"And . . . ?"

"And that same night they try to take me out in a restaurant. They miss, but there's already a bomb in my apartment. They miss again, but this time I'm long gone."

Little wheels clicked in the back of Carter's mind. His gaze strayed again to Fancy Adams on the bed. But this time he didn't look at her body. He studied her eyes, and tried to remember the bits and pieces she had told him the previous evening, between romps, about her Tokyo assignment.

Top-secret software and hardware components from top-level firms in the States, West Germany, and Japan had been finding their way into Russian hands.

Several companies were involved, but no one person could be pinned down.

Blackmail.

Charlie Loo.

"Billy . . . ?"

"Yeah, man?"

"I'll get the first flight."

"You're a lifesaver, literally," came the reply, accompanied by a deep sigh. "I'll give you all the detail stuff when you get here. I'm—"

"I know where you are. Just stay there. I'll see you in a few hours."

"I'll count every one of them on my joy stick. And, Nick . . . ?"

"Yeah?"

"Thanks."

"You got it, Billy."

Carter hung up and turned to Fancy. She shrugged and pulled the kimono over her body.

"I can read that look. It says you're not in the mood for loving," she said, belting the robe tightly around her.

"You're right. C'mon, it's coffee and conversation."

Four cups of coffee and half a pack of cigarettes later, Carter had as much as Fancy knew.

Sensitive computer parts were indeed being funneled through Japan, probably to Hong Kong and then on to the Soviet Union. She knew nothing about Charlie Loo, but by attending a lot of posh cocktail parties she had gotten close to a couple of electronics bigwigs. One of them was Ashami Okamoto. He was the chief designer for Kulo Computer Components, a division of Kulo Electronics.

At the end of her Tokyo show, Fancy had accompanied Okamoto to Hong Kong on a business trip. The people she saw him doing business with didn't look like MIT computer types.

Carter was back on the hot line.

"Ginger, is the big man in yet?"

"Yes, he just came in."

"Put me through."

"Something interesting in that Frisco call?"

"Very interesting."

Thirty seconds later, David Hawk's gruff voice came on the line. "Yes, N3, what is it? I've got N6 trying to get out of Iran."

Nick Carter laid it out in short, staccato, to-the-point sentences. As much as he could, he correlated what Billy Duong had told him to what he had learned from Fancy.

"The CIA boys are handling it, but since I've got an inside track with Billy, maybe they wouldn't mind some help."

There was a growl, a raspy cough, and a deep inhale of another lungful of cheap cigar smoke before Hawk finally answered. "Could be you've stepped into one. It's not exactly our bailiwick, but I'll call across town and see if they're interested."

"I'll be here."

Carter moved into the kitchen and poured himself another cup of coffee. "Do you have to go back to New York right away?"

"I don't *have* to do anything," Fancy replied. "Why?"

"Because you might help in San Francisco."

"On the payroll?"

"On the payroll."

"It's a deal!"

The phone rang. Over his shoulder as he headed for the bedroom, Carter heard Fancy singing "California, Here I Come," using her own dirty lyrics.

"You're onto something, N3. The Company boys have been trying to crack this for nearly a year. They would welcome your help and give you all the cooperation in the world."

"I'll give it a shot. I owe Billy Duong one anyway."

"I'll give you to Bateman."

There were a lot of whirs and clicks as the call was shifted, then Ginger came on the line.

"Your contact in San Francisco will be Mel Crompton. He'll meet you at the airport. You're under your own name on the one o'clock TWA flight out of Dulles."

"You're so efficient I'm in awe. Call 'em back and make it for two . . . F. Adams."

"The F wouldn't be for Frank, I'll bet."

"You're right."

"If I remember, F would be for a very big number just under six feet, with a lot of red hair."

"Your memory is also awe inspiring."

"Reservations for two it is. Look out, San Francisco!"

The line went dead, and Carter felt heat at his back. He turned right into Fancy's arms.

"Without going to New York, I don't have a thing to wear in San Francisco."

"What's wrong with what you wore in Tokyo and here?"

"It's worn."

Carter smiled and let her push him back across the bed. "I think my expense account will stretch."

"Good. When do we have to leave?"

"Not for an hour."

"Not much time," she murmured, "but I'll make do."

Without another word, she covered him like a soft, fleshy blanket.

TWO

It was ten o'clock, but the sun was already high and boiling down as he parked the station wagon in the mall parking lot. The lot was half full, and shoppers were scurrying from their cars to stores and back again.

He left the car's engine running, the air-conditioning vents cooling his hands as he flipped the catches on the briefcase beside him in the seat.

Inside was a Universal Enforcer Model 3000 auto carbine. The thirty-shot magazine was loaded with M1 carbine slugs, their heads slightly drilled. This was so that the slug would spread on impact, taking a lot of bone and flesh with it on its trajectory.

He inserted the magazine and jacked a shell into the chamber. When the lever action was checked, he replaced the carbine's seventeen inches into the briefcase and closed the lid.

After killing the engine, he locked the station wagon and walked across the parking lot and through the mall. Behind the stores was a narrow alleyway where trucks delivered merchandise and garbage was picked up. The alley eventually led out to a small road that circled the lake.

In dark trousers and a white polo shirt with a cardigan, he looked like a salesman making his rounds. Dark sunglasses obscured his eyes, and the face under them was deeply tanned. He was a man who spent a great deal of time in the sun.

Halfway around the lake, surrounded by trees, was a Chinese restaurant, Lu Fong's Hunan House. The rear entrance of the restaurant backed up onto the lake, the front facing a smaller artery leading off the main road that fronted the shopping center.

He paused at the edge of the trees, surveying everything carefully from behind the dark lenses.

There was an old pickup parked at the rear door. A late-model Lincoln and a foreign import were the only cars in the front parking lot.

He shunned the rear door and walked around to the front. As he passed the office, he glanced through the open slats of venetian blinds. It was empty.

The front door was unlocked. Inside, he took in the bar to his left and the dining room to his right.

There were three of them. A fat little man with sweat already staining the armpits of his fresh white shirt was restocking the bottles behind the bar.

Lu Fong, the owner.

His wife, in a Mandarin dress slit to her thighs, was at a table rolling silverware into napkins.

A wiry little man in a white T-shirt and dungarees was moving a mop listlessly across the floor of the dining room.

This was Billy Duong.

The man in the sunglasses moved to the bar. Carefully, he set the briefcase before him and took one of the stools.

"Saturday. No lunch today. Open Saturday four o'clock. You come back."

The man chuckled. "You mean there's nobody here who can even serve a cup of coffee?"

"No, no coffee. Nobody here. You come back."

The man passed a card across the bar. ''I'm with Bay Fisheries. I'd like to talk to you about cutting your expenses.''

Lu Fong appraised the card. He was always happy to cut expenses. ''We go to office, talk.''

The man watched Lu Fong walk toward the end of the bar. It was going to be perfect. Lu Fong would walk up the aisle between the bar and the tables. He would pass his wife, opening them both up for a clear burst.

The partition between the two rooms was low. He would only have to raise the barrel of the carbine six inches to reach Billy Duong with a second burst.

He unsnapped the catches on the briefcase and lifted the lid.

Lu Fong rounded the far corner of the bar and moved up the aisle. He paused and began to speak in low tones with his wife.

She nodded, and was about to answer, when thunder exploded in her ears and she saw the front of her husband's chest turn a bright crimson. She was halfway out of her chair when she realized that a hammer had struck the center of her own chest and she was being lifted from her feet and thrown backward.

She was dead by the time she hit the floor.

Billy Duong knew the sound the instant the first slug tore into Lu Fong's body. He looked up, saw the dark glasses, the tiny smile, and then the chattering carbine.

He turned and ran toward the hallway between the rest rooms that led to the rear parking lot.

Two slugs caught him in the small of the back, making him miss the hallway and crash into a booth.

He was trying to crawl back to his feet when the carbine chattered again, much closer.

He only felt one of the nine remaining slugs that tore his body practically in half.

The man rolled Billy Duong over with his foot and checked

his pulse. Satisfied, he returned to Lu Fong and his wife and did the same thing.

With the carbine back in the briefcase, he stepped over Billy Duong's body, went down the short, narrow hallway, and emerged into the sunlight.

The chattering of the carbine had been quick, and it had passed without even disturbing the birds in the trees around the lake.

A small rowboat was tied up at the pier. He shoved off, and minutes later he was halfway across the lake, at its deepest point.

It took less than ten seconds for the weighted briefcase to sink from sight, and another five minutes for the man to row the remainder of the way across the lake.

At the station wagon, he glanced at his watch.

It was 10:30.

He had a tee-off time at 11:30.

He would make it easily.

"Where?"

"Jesus, it looks like another tong war or something out here, Ward. I mean, there are three of 'em . . . the owner, his wife, and a cleanup man. Christ, all three of 'em are about cut in half!"

"I didn't say *what*, you asshole, I said *where*!"

"Out at the edge of the county, near the Plaza Shopping Center on Lakeview Road. A Chinese joint called Lu Fong's Hunan House."

"I know the place. Three of 'em, you say?"

"Yeah. There's one witness, a black guy, the dishwasher. He was in the kitchen and saw the whole thing through those little windows. You know, the kind they have in those swinging doors . . ."

"Save it. Fill me in when I get there!" He checked his watch. "I'll use the chopper . . . 'bout a half hour."

"Check."

Warden J. Christopher dropped the receiver back onto its

cradle and vigorously rubbed the knuckles of his thumbs into his eyes. They burned. But then they should. He'd had six hours of snatched catnaps in the previous two days.

Too big a case load.

Couldn't this maniac have waited until Monday to go nuts?

His right hand dropped back to the phone. He barely glanced at the instrument as his index finger poked out the well-known number.

"Hello?"

"Donnie?"

"Pop, wow, when are ya—?"

"Listen, son, let me speak to your mother."

The fingers of his free hand drummed on the desk and sweat popped out on his forehead as he waited. *Goddamned air conditioners never work when you need 'em. Just like cops, never around until you're dead. Don't worry, sir, now that we have a corpse, we'll get to the heart of this.*

"Yes?"

"Claire, it's me . . . Ward."

"I know, Ward. Your son told me."

"Yeah, Claire, I won't be able to take the kids this weekend."

The pause was interminable.

"What is it? Rape, arson, murder . . . ?"

"Claire . . ."

"Wife-beating, child-stealing, dope . . . ?"

"Claire, dammit!"

"Yes?"

"It's murder. A restaurant owner and his wife out on the lake."

Silence on the other end of the line.

"Claire, you still there?"

"Yeah."

Another pause, with audible breathing from the other end of the wire. He knew the sound. She was getting ready to explode, or. . . .

"Ward?"

"Yeah."

"Be careful."

"Yeah."

There was no good-bye. They both hung up simultaneously. They'd been doing it for years.

He made one more call.

"State Bureau hangar, Doakes."

"This is Ward Christopher. Is Lou there?"

"Yeah, Lieutenant, but just barely. He got a call from the trooper station out by the lake. They want a run up and down the coast."

"Tell him to hold it ten minutes. I need a ride."

"Will do."

He was a big, slow-moving man—two-seventy on a six-four frame. The heat that hit him outside the SBI building made him move even more slowly.

Across the street, the big digital dots on the bank sign read 98°.

Fucking humidity's probably ninety-two. What a lousy day to die.

"Carter?"

Nick Carter swiveled his head from the conveyor belt. He was a college type, about thirty, with steady eyes and set, unsmiling features. He wore the standard uniform: three-piece dark suit with a black tie and spit-shined oxfords.

"Yeah, I'm Carter."

"Mel Crompton, West Coast, Far East."

The man started to reach for ID, and Carter shook his head. "No need. This is Miss Adams."

The guy was an iceberg. When he acknowledged Fancy, he never looked below her shoulders.

"I'm afraid we've got some bad news."

"How so?"

Crompton looked at Fancy again, and shuffled.

"It's all right," Carter reassured him. "She's payroll."

Crompton almost managed a smile. "Got it on the police radio about an hour ago. Three Orientals bought it out in Marin County. Don't know for sure, but one of them might be your man. Place called Lu Fong's . . ."

"That's the place," Carter growled, not trying to hide the anger and despair that he knew had blossomed on his face. "Know any details?"

"No, sir."

"You have a driver?"

"Yes, sir."

"I'll take your car," Carter said. "You take my bags and Miss Adams. Where are we staying?"

"We have a Company condo on the bay, just south of the city."

"Good. Show me your car!"

As usual, there was a solid gasp and a total rollover in Ward Christopher's ample belly when the copter lifted off, spun in midair, and dipped forward to fly. He was pretty sure that the pilot, Lou Jenkins, speeded up all those maneuvers just for his benefit.

It was common knowledge around the State Bureau of Investigation that Christopher was scared to death of anything mechanical that moved, earthbound or airborne. He wouldn't even ride in an automobile unless he drove, and that was usually between thirty-five and forty miles per hour.

He was even afraid of boats.

"Think it's some kind of nut?" Jenkins shouted over the whirring rotor and roaring engine.

"Yeah, sounds like it."

"What's with these guys? They gotta be crazy."

"They're all a little crazy, Lou. They get liquored up, or doped up, or wigged out on kicks . . . all they need is a gun and somebody to point it at to get their rocks off."

"Jesus, it ain't like the old days. At least Dillinger did it for money. Cra-zy."

Christopher didn't want to talk; he wanted to think. He leaned his thick mop of gray-streaked black hair against the barely padded headrest and closed his eyes.

Warden Jerry Christopher, fifty years old, twenty-five years a cop. He'd made detective after just six years on a city force. Four years later, a citation from the governor had brought him to the attention of the State Bureau of Investigation.

"Fifteen years . . ."

"Huh?"

"Just thinkin'. I've been with the SBI fifteen years. Hard years."

"I only got six in, but hell, things are a hell of a lot easier up here than down there."

"Yeah," Christopher said, sticking a dry pipe in his mouth and wishing it were a cigarette, "they are."

The chopper lurched sideways and then rolled.

"Goddamn, Lou, do you have to do that?"

"Sorry, Ward," Jenkins said with a grin as he leveled the copter out and idled back. Christopher was sure he wasn't sorry at all. But then, needling Ward Christopher was a pleasant way for everyone in the Bureau to break the boredom. And the big lieutenant was an all-around nice guy who would take it.

"There's the lake . . . restaurant's over there. I'll let you out in that vacant lot."

"Thanks. You got a cigarette, Lou?"

"Yeah. Thought you quit . . . ulcers or something."

"I did."

The copter nosed over, and Christopher felt as if he were going down the first hill on the Hurricane out at Playland Park. He hated Playland Park. He'd only taken the kids there once.

The machine landed with a bounce, and Christopher slid from the passenger side with the rotors still turning. He was barely clear when Lou Jenkins lifted off again, nearly flattening him with the wash from the rotors.

"Bastard," Christopher mumbled, then crossed the vacant lot.

He hefted his bulk over a wire fence and crossed the hard-packed dirt road to the restaurant's parking lot. It was quiet, and country sounds were floating up from the lake. Even the noisy whirr of katydids and the croaking of frogs were somehow peaceful. But the feeling diminished the closer he got to the restaurant's square, squat building.

The conversation, technical sounds, and general hubbub coming from the open windows were all too familiar.

"Get a shot here, of his head . . . and then another of the rest of it here on the wall."

Christopher winced.

"Lieutenant, glad you're here. I've got notes on everything . . ."

His name was Milo Ferris. He was the youngest sergeant in the Special Bureau, and also the smartest. His major problem, as far as Ward Christopher was concerned, was how he so thoroughly enjoyed being efficient.

Christopher ground out his cigarette, nodding every now and then as Ferris filled him in.

The slugs were powerful, probably from an army-issue M1, or even an M16. They were also doctored to up their kill ratio. None of the three victims lived more than a few seconds.

"Anything taken?"

"No, sir," Ferris intoned. "The witness, one Randolph D. Brown, dishwasher, says the guy didn't even hit the cash register or do a search. He just killed and walked away."

Christopher sighed. "Rules out robbery . . ."

"Yes, sir, my guess exactly. Do you think it could be a tong war, Lieutenant?"

"Ferris, I don't know what the hell to think. Where is he?"

"Who, sir?"

"The dishwasher, dammit."

"Oh. In the back. He's scared to death, still shaking."

"I would imagine," Christopher nodded, moving toward the kitchen doors.

"Uh, Lieutenant . . ."

"Yeah?"

Ferris moved up beside him, close enough so Christopher could smell the coffee on his breath.

"There's a Fed here wants to talk to you."

"A what?"

"A Fed."

"FBI?"

"Uh, no."

"What then?"

"I don't know. He's right over there."

Christopher rolled his eyes without moving his head, his police brain quickly cataloguing the man he saw: hard eyes, vacant face, tanned skin, about six-foot-two and built like an athlete.

He wore a tan suit that was perfectly cut to hide the piece under his left armpit to any but a trained eye.

"I'll see him after I talk to the witness."

Ferris paled. "Uh, Lieutenant, he says he wants to talk to you . . . now."

"Oh he does, does he?"

Christopher jammed his dry pipe between his teeth and crossed the room.

"I'm Lieutenant Ward Christopher. Let's see some ID."

"Of course, Lieutenant. The name's Nick Carter, special detail, Immigration."

Carter passed him one of the many IDs he carried for just such an occasion. AXE operatives could be anyone from a U.S. Treasury agent to a diplomatic attaché just by using the proper ID they constantly carried.

Christopher did everything but hold the card up to the light, then passed it back.

"Okay, I'll give you everything as soon as I get it."

Carter shook his head. "I want everything firsthand, Lieutenant."

"Screw you."

"I think we'd better talk."

Christopher had the other man by fifty pounds, easy, but the fingers on his arm moved him like a feather. When they were several feet from Milo Ferris and two uniformed patrolmen, the grip released.

"Look, Carter, I'm sick and tired of you federal bastards comin' in—"

"Save it! I'm not here to horn in on your investigation. I can cut through a lot of crap for you if you'll let me, but I want your cooperation in return."

"And if I don't give it?"

"I can usurp your authority with one phone call."

Christopher studied the intense dark eyes for several seconds. Then his cop's intuition told him that this man, Carter, meant every word he said.

"Okay, what have you got?"

"It was a professional hit. The real target was the cleanup man. I don't know what name he was using here in the States, but his real name was Billy Duong. Recently, he was working for an outfit in Tokyo called Kulo Electronics under the name of William Soo Luong."

"It can be traced," Christopher said. "Was he one of yours?"

"No, but we think he was onto something big that we can use. I want a look at his personal effects and an hourly rundown on what you find."

Christopher felt a lot better. This guy was for real.

"You've got it," he said with a nod. "Let's go talk to the witness."

Randolph D. Brown was about eighteen years old, tall enough to reach a basketball hoop without going to his toes, and still shaking like a leaf.

"Cool, I mean that mother was like ice! He just hauls out

this gun and *bam, bam, bam, bam* . . ."

"All right, Mr. Brown, can you just tell me everything you saw."

The young black man went over it in about ten minutes, and then Christopher had him go through it all twice more. When that was done, the lieutenant started into detailed questions.

Carter, true to his word, stayed in the background, listening and smoking.

At last Christopher looked up at Carter, the question in his eyes, "Anything you want to ask?"

The answer was "No," also given with just the eyes, and the two men returned to the dining room.

Carter was the first to speak. "The weapon he described sounds like a machine pistol of some kind. From the size, maybe a Stechkin."

"That's Russian, isn't it?"

Carter nodded. "Yeah, but the Stechkin won't take M1 slugs. However, there's a 3000 auto carbine called the Universal Enforcer that will."

"You know your armament."

"Part of my business," Carter stated flatly. "But I'm not a cop. What did you get out of Brown's ranting?"

"Something, maybe," Christopher replied, sucking on his dry pipe. "He said the killer was short, wiry, with straight black hair. He wore sunglasses, so Brown couldn't see his eyes, but if this is a professional hit, and if your man was the target . . ."

"The killer was probably Oriental," Carter offered.

"Right. Something else struck me. Brown noticed that his right hand was darker than his left. Also, there was a thin line of lighter skin around his hairline on his forehead."

Carter puzzled this for a moment, then shrugged. "You've got me."

"A golf glove."

"What?"

"The guy wears a golf glove. He's right-handed, so he

wears the glove on his left hand when he plays.''

"So his right hand would get all the sun . . .''

"Right. Also, a visor would shield part of his forehead!''

Carter smiled. "You're a good cop, Christopher. So we've got a killer who's a golfer, probably an Oriental, and maybe is connected to an electronics outfit.''

"I'll get my people on it right away.''

"Good. In the meantime, I'd like to go through Billy Duong's things in his room.''

"I'll have Ferris give you a hand.''

"You mean watch me to make sure I give you everything I get?''

"You might say that,'' Christopher said and grinned.

It was a cubbyhole of a room, half storage, half living quarters, with a table, a couple of chairs, and a cot.

They found all of Billy Duong's possessions, other than a few clothes, in a seabag.

"Not much here.''

"Not much,'' Carter agreed, "but maybe enough.''

The passport was phony, under a phony name. There were three letters postmarked Hong Kong, from Lin Duong.

Carter guessed this was the sister that Billy Duong had mentioned.

The letters were dated about a month apart. The first two were just newsy, but there was some meat in the last one dated only two weeks before.

> I found the address of the woman about whom you inquire, Connie Chu. It is Number 18 Kowloon Road. She must be very rich to live in such a place, Brother. From her manservant, I find out that she owns junks, and is also the proprietor of a gambling house in Macao, the Hungry Dragon.
>
> I will try to find out the last of what you require and send it in my next letter.

Carter smiled. Now he knew that Charlie Loo was involved, and that Billy Duong was digging pretty deep.

At one time, Connie had been a part-time ally of Loo. If anyone in the world could get in touch with Charlie Loo, it would probably be Connie Chu.

"Get these copied for me, will you, Ferris?"

"Sure thing, sir."

Carter returned to the dining room. The mess was almost cleaned up, and outside they were putting up blockades and signs reading NO TRESPASSING—POLICE INVESTIGATION.

He checked out with Christopher, gave him the number and address of the Company condo, and found his car and driver.

It was a two-hour ride across the bridge and down the peninsula.

The condo was one of four, very posh, and sitting on a cliff overlooking the sea. When he found out that it came with a Company car, Carter dismissed the driver.

"Crompton's still here. I'll wait for him."

"Right."

Halfway up the path, Crompton met him. "A mess?"

"A big one," Carter said tightly. "I'm calling Washington. Chances are I'll take the heat from here on."

The other man's face evidenced relief. "Suits us just fine," he said, and then chuckled. "Your lady's been shopping. She's inside."

When Carter walked into the apartment, Fancy was modeling.

"You like?"

"What's it setting my expense account back?"

"A little over fifteen hundred," she said, shrugging.

"Leave it on. We'll celebrate your newfound wealth over dinner."

Carter poured himself three fingers of Chivas and found the telephone. Ginger Bateman picked up on the second ring and put him right through to Hawk.

Carter machine-gunned the day's events, then waited while Hawk thought them through.

"I've had a couple more conversations with the crowd across town," Hawk growled. "They're more than happy to dump it in our laps, especially since you know Charlie Loo."

"Do I stay on it, then?"

"All the way. What's your plan of attack?"

"A couple of days here, just in case the locals can turn up something on the killer, and then Hong Kong and probably Tokyo."

"I'll alert the British in Hong Kong and our friends in Tokyo. It sounds as though you'll need all the help you can get."

"I'll stay in touch."

Carter had barely replaced the phone when it rang.

"Yes?"

"Carter, please."

"Speaking."

"Christopher here. We may be in luck. A bunch of the computer geniuses from down south in Silicon Valley are having a little convention with their Japanese and German counterparts."

"Where?"

"They're spread out over two golf resorts, Sea Cliffs and the Alhambra. It's a two-day tournament, today and tomorrow, with a welcoming dinner tonight at the Alhambra."

"Is that close to where I am?"

"About ten minutes. I can get us a table."

"Do it. Make it for three."

"Three?"

"Right. There's a lady with me who has been in on this. It's just a hunch, but she may have seen this guy's face in Japan or Hong Kong."

"Anything that'll help. See you in an hour."

Fancy entered the bedroom just as the connection broke.

"Where do we eat?"

Carter answered her question with one of his own. "Think you could recognize any of the people you saw with Okamoto in Hong Kong if you saw them again?"

"Sure. Why?"

"Just a hunch. You're on the payroll, remember? We're going country clubbing!"

THREE

The telephone booth was in the pool area, and with the door closed it was stifling. Perspiration was already seeping through his dress shirt beneath the dinner jacket as he waited for the overseas operator to make the connection.

The booth could be seen from the club's main dining room, so he had unscrewed the bulb. Every now and then he glanced up at the tall windows. It was an outside chance, but the red-headed woman just might come out for a breath of air while he was making the call.

"*Hai?*"

"The situation has been remedied."

"Excellent, but there is perhaps a new change in plans. I have just received a call from my contact with Japanese security here in Tokyo."

"Yes?"

"A federal agent from Washington has been assigned to the case. I know him from years ago. His name is Nick Carter. He is in San Francisco now, and will be coming to Tokyo soon according to my source. I don't want him to arrive in Tokyo."

Little bells went off in the back of the man's mind. At first he had thought that the appearance of the tall redhead might be a coincidence. Now he knew differently.

"Describe this man Carter to me."

He listened, nodding his head, and now and then glancing up at the windows as Charlie Loo described to perfection one of the two men sitting with the redhead.

"This man is here, at the golf club, right now. He is with the whore who accompanied Okamoto to Hong Kong on the last run."

"Then she, too, must be an agent, and Okamoto must be compromised. That means there will be further work for you when you return home."

"I will take care of the problem yet this evening."

The connection was broken without a farewell. None was needed.

He slipped from the booth and walked around the pool, being careful to stay outside the light from the dining room windows. The resort's grounds were vast, with over two hundred rooms in the main hotel buildings and just under one hundred cabanas scattered across manicured lawns and graveled paths.

When he reached his cabana, he went inside and immediately began to strip out of his formal wear. In place of it, he donned a black turtleneck sweater and a pair of dark trousers.

It might be coincidence that this man Carter and the big-breasted woman were in the club dining room, but if it weren't, it meant that they were onto something.

The second man at the table with them had "policeman" written all over him.

But if they knew his identity, surely they would be arresting him instead of calmly eating dinner.

That meant they were fishing.

He picked up the phone in the cabana and dialed the main desk.

"May I help you?"

"Yes, could I have Mr. Nick Carter's room, please?"

"One moment." The operator was back in seconds. "I'm sorry, sir, but there is no one by that name registered."

"I see. Thank you."

He eased the instrument back onto its cradle and tented his fingers in front of his face in thought.

Using his golfing background as a cover for this assignment had been a mistake. Particularly in a tournament with such a large group of men who were both Orientals and in the electronics business.

Obviously, Billy Duong had somehow contacted this man Carter. All he could hope for was that Duong had not revealed everything before his life had ended.

In any event, removing Carter and the woman would do away with the problem.

He removed his spare set of clubs from the closet, and carefully took the heads from the driver and the three wood. Inside the thin veneer covering were two powerful hand grenades.

From the false bottom of the bag, he took a Ruger .357 magnum. He placed the grenades and the gun in the middle of some towels in his locker bag, and exited the cabana.

He retrieved his rented car from the parking lot and drove around the long, horseshoe-shaped drive, pulling the car to a halt and parking about a hundred yards from the club's main entrance.

From where he sat, he could see everyone leaving.

The meal was forgettable, the entertainment more so. Conversation consisted of a look and a word here and there.

Carter had filled Fancy in on the short ride down the coast, so most of her time was spent rubbernecking every Oriental man in the room. That meant nearly a hundred faces.

By ten the party was breaking up and they had gotten nowhere.

"Want to call it a night?" Ward Christopher asked at last. "We can start in the morning on the first tee. That is, if you think Miss Adams may really be able to spot our man."

Carter sighed and nodded. "You're pretty sure Brown, the dishwasher, wouldn't be able to identify him?"

"I'm sure. He wore those big, aviator-type glasses, and most of the time his face was turned away from the kitchen door windows."

"If we're leaving," Fancy said, rising, "I'm going to freshen up."

Carter nodded again. "I'll get the check. We'll meet you at the front door."

Both of them watched her move through the tables, and then Christopher chuckled. "Pretty lady."

"Very," Carter said, rising, "and smart."

They paid the bill and moved into the club's large foyer. Christopher passed his car stub to a runner, then turned to Carter. "I don't suppose you'd care to enlighten me a little further on what's behind all this."

Carter lit a cigarette and thought. He liked and trusted this police lieutenant. The man was not only a good cop, he was also a savvy one. On impulse, he decided to give Christopher at least the framework.

By the time he had finished, Christopher's already hooded eyes were nearly closed. "Out of my league," he said. "If it's all that big, this guy is a real pro. I doubt we'll have a chance at him."

"You're probably right, and if we did get him, I doubt if he knows who actually hired him."

The car arrived and sat idling at the bottom of the steps. Fancy joined them a moment later, and the three of them rode in silence back to the condo.

"Want to come in for a nightcap?"

Christopher shrugged. "Why not?"

Walking to the door, Carter noticed that the cop's seamed face was drawn and his movements were abrupt and jerky, as if his muscles were not responding properly.

"How long have you been a cop, Christopher?"

"Too long. How long have you been . . . whatever you are?"

Carter smiled. "Long enough to have used up about seven of my nine lives."

Fancy shuddered and they entered the big apartment.

"I'm going to change," she said and veered off into the bedroom.

"You know, of course, that we'll never get this guy," Christopher said, lowering his big frame into a sofa.

"I'll get him," Carter replied. "If not here, somewhere. What would you like to drink?"

"Anything . . . brandy, if you've got it."

"Coming up."

The drinks were poured and Fancy was just entering the room when the window to Carter's left exploded. A shiny object sailed by his head and landed on the carpet in the middle of the room.

All three of them were mesmerized as they watched what looked like the head of a golf club roll directly toward the sofa where Chistopher sat.

Suddenly Carter's training and sixth sense clicked in.

"Grenade!" he shouted and dropped like a rock to the floor.

The blast was like the thunder of a battleship's sixteen-inch guns in the closed room. Carter felt the floor heave, and then the bar fell in on him as the glass and bottles behind it exploded.

Sharp pains knifed at the back of his head, his neck, and his legs. It took a full minute for his head to clear from the shock of the concussion, and another two minutes to disentangle himself from the rubble of the bar.

The room was a complete wreck. The furniture had been turned into kindling, and there was a gaping hole in the floor directly below where the sofa had been.

The sofa itself was in shreds, and so was Ward Christopher.

Carter could see with one look that the man was dead.

Fancy Adams was a different story. The housecoat and gown beneath had practically been torn from her body, and the body itself was a mass of tiny splinter wounds all gushing blood.

But she was alive.

Carter probed the pockets of what was left of Christopher's jacket until he found the car keys. He then yanked a curtain from the window and rolled Fancy into it. The last thing he did before sweeping her up into his arms was fill his right hand with the 9mm Luger, Wilhelmina, from the shoulder rig under his jacket.

It was ten-to-one that the bomber was long gone, but there was always that one chance.

He burst through the shattered door and ran, with the woman in his arms, toward the car.

Lights were coming on in all the neighboring buildings, and a few people stood gaping in their open doorways.

All in one motion, he set Fancy in the car, slapped the red light on the roof, and started the engine. In seconds, he was screaming down the street and flipping buttons until he got the radio working.

When he got a voice, he pressed the "send" button on the hand mike.

"There has been a bombing at Nine-eleven Cliffside Drive. Lieutenant Warden Christopher is dead. I am a federal officer, Nicholas Carter. I have a wounded female and am driving Christopher's car. Am on Ocean Drive heading north. Where do I turn to get to Memorial Hospital?"

The radio crackled, and a brisk, efficient, and calm female voice came back at him. "Turn right at Chester, go five blocks away from the ocean, and you'll see the hospital."

"Check. Have Sergeant Milo Ferris meet me at the hospital, and dispatch a team to the Cliffside address. No reporters

. . . I repeat, *no* reporters. The building is a CIA safe house.''

An acknowledgment came through, and Carter floored the accelerator.

"Yeah, some safe house," he hissed aloud, throwing a quick glance at the other seat.

Fancy's face, where it wasn't caked with drying blood, was pale white. Most of her hair and her eyebrows were gone. He fumbled his fingers at her throat, and when he could find no pulse, he laid his hand on her chest.

She was still breathing, but barely.

Ten minutes later he skidded to a halt in front of the hospital's emergency entrance. He was just scooping her up, when four white-coated figures pulling a gurney came bursting through the door.

"I'm Dr. Hagen. We'll take her."

"It's probably a concussion," Carter rasped. "The cuts are probably steel fragments and wood splinters, maybe some glass."

They already had Fancy on the gurney and headed toward the door. One of the men turned and wound his arm around Carter's shoulder.

"Can you make it inside, walking?"

"Hell, yes, why not?"

"Man, you're dripping blood like a sieve."

Carter brushed the back of his neck with his hand. It came away bathed in red.

"I'll be damned."

He took two steps and passed out in the intern's arms.

He came to, naked, facedown on a padded table. A young, attractive nurse was standing at his head, passing things to hands that worked on his body.

"How am I?"

"You had about a pound of glass in you, from your head to your toes," a gruff male voice said. "And you had two very serious wounds full of wood splinters. About forty stitches took care of it. I'm going to put you back to sleep for a little bit."

"A police sergeant is on his way here . . . Milo Ferris. I want to be awake to talk to him when he arrives."

"You will be."

Carter felt the bite of a needle, and then he was out again.

He blinked once, twice, three times, and then his eyes stayed open.

This time he was facedown in a bed in a hospital gown. Gray dawn oozed through a window, and every part of his body felt as though it were on fire.

Out of the corner of his eye, he saw Milo Ferris sitting by the bed. The same nurse who had been handing things earlier was standing in the doorway, wide-eyed.

"Well?" Carter asked.

"The grenade was a modified M-80. We found some odd wood fragments in the shrapnel . . ."

"It was disguised as a golf club . . . the head of a wood. Christopher?"

"He never knew what hit him."

"Miss Adams?"

"She died about an hour ago."

"Son of a bitch. Nurse!"

"Yes, sir . . ."

"Get out! And close the door behind you!"

She moved like a scalded cat.

Ferris was on his feet. "We have no real leads, other than the golf connection. I've got a team ready to interrogate all the Orientals this morning."

"No."

"What the hell do you mean, Carter? Ward Christopher is dead! This is our baby now!"

"I know how you feel, Ferris, but this can't be handled by the book anymore. Can we still make the morning news?"

Ferris was a strong-willed man and a good cop, but Carter's ferocity cowed him. "Yeah, I can arrange it."

"Do that. I want you to release a statement that Christopher was killed in the blast. Miss Adams and I survived until we reached the hospital. We both died without regaining consciousness. Got all that?"

"Yes."

"Good. Swear all these doctors and nurses to secrecy, even if you have to tag an unclaimed corpse with my name for a while. Also, let it slip to the media that revenge is suspected as a motive. Call it underworld terror or some such garbage. Get a man out to the condo to pick up my clothes. Tell him to stop by a wig salon on his way back. Take notes!"

Ferris whipped out a pad and copied down all the items as Carter ticked them off. "Anything else?"

"Yeah. Pick up the Alhambra's manager and whoever is in charge of the golf tournament. Tell 'em nothing, and get 'em down here!"

"I'm on my way."

"Wait a minute. Put that phone beside my head."

"I don't know what you're planning," Ferris said, moving the phone, "but the docs say you can't get out of here for a week."

"What do they know? Move!"

The door had barely closed behind Ferris when the phone started ringing in Ginger Bateman's Arlington apartment.

A sleepy voice mumbled "Hello" into the phone, and Carter chuckled.

"I figured you'd still be in bed."

"Why shouldn't I be? It's Sunday morning. Nick?"

"Yeah."

"Where are you?"

"In a hospital. Fancy Adams is dead."

"Oh, no!"

"Yeah. And the noon news back there is going to tell you that I am also very dead. Get on the horn to the big man and tell him to follow it through.''

"You've got it. How does he reach you?''

"He doesn't, for a while. I'll be back in touch from Hong Kong or Tokyo, depending how the work goes tonight. If you need any more info, there's a local cop who's in on it, a Sergeant Milo Ferris.''

"Check.''

"Later.''

He hung up the phone just as the cute little nurse walked through the door.

"Is there anything I can get you, sir?''

"Did the sergeant clue you in?''

"Yes, sir. Admissions is changing your records right now.''

"How many people on this floor know the truth?''

"Only myself, an intern, and the doctor who treated you.''

"Make sure it stays that way.''

"Yes, sir.''

"And bring me four eggs over easy, a steak, some potatoes, and a pot of coffee.''

"But that's not on the menu. I—''

"Bring it in from outside then,'' Carter growled. "What the hell, I'm dead anyway. Who's to know?''

FOUR

Nick Carter's mood was both weary and excited as he drove into the country club's private parking compound and turned the rented car over to an attendant.

It was midafternoon, and the morning heat had been replaced by a light breeze and an overcast sky. In the west, over the ocean, a faint stain of lemon-yellow light flickered in feeble contrast to the grayness of the immense white clubhouse and the ultragreen fairways.

Inside the massive lobby, Carter paused to check his new appearance in an antique, walnut-framed mirror.

The spirit-gum-induced and eyebrow-shaded wrinkles in his face were holding up well, as was the gray mustache that had been introduced to his upper lip. Beneath the matching gray wig, his completely sheared scalp itched a little from the razor's touch.

"Are you sure, sir?" the young nurse had said, shocked by his request.

"I'm sure. Shave it . . . all of it. Make me as bald as a billiard ball, honey."

She had nicked his aching pate only twice in the process, which Carter was thankful for.

He adjusted his well-tailored jacket, touched his tie, and strolled through the dining room into the club's lounge. The room's darkness was relieved only by low, shaded lamps on the tables and a generally diffused glow from the region of the bar. Somewhere, a piano tinkled a subdued background for the hum of voices.

He spotted Jules Monroe in a rear booth and headed his way.

Monroe was one of the two men Milo Ferris had rounded up that morning and brought to the hospital. He was the public relations rep who had organized the convention and the golf tournament.

The other man had been Colin MacIntyre, a crusty old Scot, who was the resort manager. It was MacIntyre who had voiced the biggest objections to Carter's demands.

"We are an old and respected hotel and club, sir. I protest. We cannot intrude upon our guests' privacy in such a way!"

"My dear MacIntyre," Carter had replied, trying tact first, "I respect that, but this is murder."

"No matter. To allow you to spy upon our guests—"

"Mr. MacIntyre, if I'm not given the cooperation I'm asking for, it's going to be much worse for all your guests."

"What do you mean?"

"I'll close down your little golf tournament, closet your guests in their rooms, and interrogate them one by one. That could take days."

Colin MacIntyre had quickly agreed.

Carter oozed his aching backside into the booth opposite Jules Monroe and winced as he pulled out his cigarette case.

"I'm sorry, sir, but you'll have to take another table. I'm waitng—"

"It's okay, Monroe. It's me."

"Good God . . ."

"Amazing, isn't it?" Carter smiled. "What have you got?"

Monroe unsnapped a briefcase sitting on the seat beside him and removed a few papers. He carefully laid them out on the table, then studied them with a frowning forehead. His otherwise smooth face, with its neatly clipped mustache, was vacuous and resigned in the glow of the table lamp.

Carter pegged him as a man who could display a certain charm at times, and just as easily retreat inscrutably behind the lenses of his plastic-rimmed glasses when he deemed it necessary.

"There are five men who fit the general outline you gave me this morning at the hospital."

He was about to flip the papers around on the table, when a waitress arrived, holding a glass pot of hot coffee.

"Would you care for a drink, sir?"

"No, I'll just have some of that coffee if you don't mind."

She poured him a cup, smiled, and left.

Carter flipped through the papers. They were fairly comprehensive rundowns on the men that Monroe had selected based on Carter's specifications. The specifications themselves were mostly hunches on Carter's part, but his past experiences in dealing with professional hit men gave him an inside track.

In this instance, the man would most likely be Oriental, small in stature, a man who played golf a great deal and who probably had used the golf tournament as a cover for going after Billy Duong. He would also be single, traveling alone, a frugal tipper, and an expensive but conservative dresser.

People who kill for a living like to spend their money on good things but don't like to draw attention to themselves by throwing it around.

The men described on the five sheets of paper in front of Carter fulfilled every item on the list.

Carter sighed. "Okay, let's dig a little deeper. How many of these five didn't attend the banquet last night?"

Monroe consulted the notebook in his hand, scanned his

eyes over the sheets, and pulled one of them toward him.

"Those four all attended the cocktail party, but not the dinner."

Carter nodded. That would fit in with his theory that the killer had spotted Fancy, recognized her, and knew she would recognize him if she saw him in the dining room.

Carter went over the specs on the four, and then over them again. Finally he raised his eyes to Monroe.

"Two of these guys are golf pros in Japan."

"That's right. We frequently invite a couple of pros from each member country. It kind of spices up the tournament. They are usually sponsored by one or more of the participating companies."

"Do you know who sponsored these two?"

"No, I don't, but I can find out."

"Do," Carter said. "And while you're at it, check the hotel records and find out how and when these guys are leaving when this shindig is over."

"Will do."

"Do you have the pairings and tee-off times for them?"

Monroe nodded and scribbled on his pad. When he was finished, he passed the paper to Carter, as well as a layout of the course.

"They're not paired together, of course. Osami would be here about now, and Komuku would be at about the fourteenth hole."

"Good. Can you fix me up with an official's jacket and a golf cart? I want to get a look at them."

"A look . . . ?"

"That's right," Carter said with a smile. "I have kind of a sixth sense when it comes to spotting a man who kills other men. It's in the eyes."

Carter didn't add that it takes one to know one.

For the next hour Carter played Course Ranger, shuttling

the golf cart back and forth between the two groups of golfers.

Both men were definitely "inscrutable Oriental" types. In fact, they could have been clones of one another. Several times he was able to get close to both Kiki Osami and Ishi Komuku, and nothing in their manner or the way they looked physically gave his instincts the tumble they needed.

Finally he gave up, decided to try a last-ditch guess, and headed back for the eighteenth green.

He knew that given enough time and manpower, Milo Ferris and the rest of the police department could piece together the kind of info that would nail their prey.

But Carter didn't have that kind of time.

He found Monroe in the scorer's tent and guided him to the outside and privacy.

"They're both leaving tomorrow," Monroe murmured. "Osami to Tokyo on the noon Pan Am, and Komuku on the two-fifteen flight to Hong Kong."

Carter nodded, his mind going ninety miles an hour. It could still be either one of them, since Charlie Loo could be operating out of either place.

He popped the big question. "Who sponsored them in the tournament?"

"Let me see . . ." Monroe consulted his ever-present note pad and looked back at Carter. "Kulo Electronics sponsored both of them."

"Damn," Carter said.

"But there is one thing . . ."

"What?"

"Komuku was a last-minute replacement."

"Oh?"

"Yeah. A pro named Nodame had a motorcycle accident outside Tokyo, and Komuku was rushed in to take his place."

The wheels clicked in Carter's brain.

"What's Komuku's room number?"

"No room. He's in one of the cabanas. He insisted on a single room away from the others."

Bingo, Carter thought, and grabbed Monroe's arm so hard and quickly that the other man jumped.

"Get me a key to that cabana."

"Jesus, Carter, MacIntyre will—"

"Get it!"

Carter cased every inch of the doorframe before he inserted the key and let himself into the cabana.

The bed, other furniture, and practically empty bags yielded nothing.

There were two closets. Again, he checked around the door of the first one before opening it.

It was empty.

Carter was just as cautious before he dived into the second.

Komuku's clothes were mostly sporty, with a couple of expensively tailored summer suits, custom-made shirts, and silk ties to complete his wardrobe. Almost all the clothing had labels bearing the name of a Hong Kong tailor.

Carter made a mental note of it, then went through the pockets. Nothing, not even a handkerchief or a book of matches.

The guy was meticulous, even down to the way the hangers all pointed the same way.

The only other items in the closet were a small traveling bag and an extra set of golf clubs. The small bag contained a warm-up suit, some jogging shoes, and two pairs of squeezers for wrist and grip conditioning.

Carter was about to grab the golf bag, when his hand froze.

There was a long black hair finely threaded through a seam in the handle and pasted to the closet wall, probably with saliva.

It could have been an accident or coincidence, but the Killmaster didn't think so.

With a tender hand, he took the bag of clubs from the closet, being careful to disengage the hair from only the wall and not from the grip.

Old habits die hard, he thought, smiling, *and usually they don't die at all*.

The pockets produced only the usual golfer's paraphernalia: balls, tees, markers, some Band-Aids, and an extra pair of shoes.

From the markings, almost everything had been purchased from the Hitaga Country Club, near Kobi in Japan.

Finished with the pockets, he rezipped them and, one by one, removed the clubs.

It took him fifteen minutes to minutely examine each one, and he was rewarded with absolutely nothing.

"Damn," he muttered, "the bastard didn't mark this bag for nothing!"

Only when he replaced the clubs did he notice something odd. They didn't go all the way to the bottom of the bag. And, measuring with one of them, he discovered that if they did, the heads wouldn't reach over the top.

Odd, he thought, that would make it very difficult for a golfer to easily pull them out.

It took him less than a minute to find the catch that released the false bottom in the golf bag.

But even its presence wasn't conclusive proof. Everyone who traveled as much as Komuku probably did, practiced a little bit of smuggling.

Nevertheless, the false compartment was one more check on the plus side that Komuku was his man, even when he found it empty.

He put the bag back in the closet and was about to replace the hair with his own saliva, when he remembered something else. There were two loose head covers in the pockets. He checked them, and found the numerals 1 and 3 embossed in gold stitching into the leather. There were two woods in the bag, a 4 and a 5.

Carter was no golfer, but he knew a little about the game and its tools. The number 1 wood was a driver, to be used off the tee. The number 3 wood was the longest distance club in the fairway.

No golfer—let alone a pro—would be running around without those two clubs.

Hurriedly, he set everything back the way he had found it and exited the cabana, locking the door behind him.

Komuku was on the eighteenth green by the time Carter got back. He found Monroe pacing nervously beside the scorer's tent.

"Jesus," the man sighed, his face an open mask of relief, "I'm glad you made it back. My brain's mush trying to find a way of keeping him here. Did you find anything?"

"Maybe, maybe not. You know many golfers that carry only two woods in their bags, a four and a five?"

"You mean, no driver?"

"Yeah, and no three wood."

"Maybe, but it would be rare. He'd probably be a real duffer that would sacrifice distance for accuracy. Maybe even use an iron off the tee."

"But no pro?"

"No way."

"And Komuku is a pro."

Monroe nodded. "He's not in the big leagues, of course, but, yeah, he's definitely a pro."

Carter was already moving away. "Stay here! I'll be right back!"

He joined the crowd around the green. Komuku had already putted out and was standing with his caddie near the edge of the break in the crowd that led to the scorer's tent, waiting for his playing partner to finish.

Carter edged his way through the people until he could practically touch the man.

He glanced down at Komuku's golf bag where the caddie held it loosely between his hands.

There were four woods in the bag, and two of them were definitely a driver and a number 3 wood.

As gently as possible, Carter elbowed his way into the clear and moved back toward Monroe's waiting figure.

It wasn't a sure thing, mostly supposition, but it would be enough to have Milo Ferris come in and lump Komuku with Osami and two or three others for intensive questioning. The chances were decent that with enough probing, Komuku could be held and even linked on circumstantial evidence.

But that would take time, too much time.

And if it were Komuku, he would be warned. Carter wanted him loose and with his mind free. There had to be a way to make Komuku tip his hand without knowing that he did it.

"Monroe . . .?"

"What now?"

"Give me an itinerary . . . what you know, and what you guess Komuku might do between now and tomorrow at two-fifteen when his flight leaves for Hong Kong."

"You think he's the one?"

"I'm guessing," Carter replied with a shrug. "Not much else I can do at this stage of the game. What have you got?"

Monroe thought for a moment and then smiled. "I know for sure one thing he'll be doing."

"What's that?"

"Attending the lawn party and banquet around the pool tonight."

"How can you be sure?"

"He just won the tournament. It ain't the P.G.A., but first place does pay ten grand. I'm sure he'll show up to collect."

Carter paced for a full five minutes and then nearly whooped. He had it, almost the perfect way.

"Get a room in the hotel. In fact, make it a two-bedroom suite!"

"Christ, man, I can't just . . ."

But Carter was already halfway up the path toward the

clubhouse and a telephone.

He got through to information in the Los Angeles area and quickly obtained the number of *Sport Times* magazine. He then dialed direct and punched change into the slot at the operator's command.

"Lewiston Publications, L.A. office."

"Barney Riley, please. He's with *Sport Times*."

"Yes, sir. One moment, please."

Years before, Barney Riley had taken two good cracks at the middleweight championship. He had always been a good fighter, but never quite *that* good. He had lost both matches and then quit.

No dummy, he'd gotten himself an education and become a sportswriter. Carter and Riley had crossed paths a couple of times, the main one being when Riley was investigating some fixed fights in Miami, and the fixers had turned out to be connected with a bunch of doperunners out of Cuba.

Carter had been trying to cancel the doperunners. It worked out that he and Riley ended up joining forces to achieve the same ends.

The man had proved to be a smart and capable ally in a pinch.

"Yeah, Riley here."

"Barney, can you still throw a right like you can bend an elbow off a bar?"

"Who the hell is this?"

"Miami, 'seventy-four, Antonio Gonzalez. You broke his jaw with one punch, and I stuffed some white powder down his throat so he wouldn't wake up."

"Carter?"

"No one else."

"Jesus, man, you're dead! It's all over the tube, and you even made page three of the *Times* down here!"

"Just goes to show cops and federal officers don't rate very high."

"Then you're alive?"

"Very much so, Barney, but I probably did use up another of my lives. I need a favor . . . maybe a big one."

"For you, anything."

"How soon can you get to San Francisco?"

"Three hours at the most. What's up?"

"I want you to do a piece of acting, a lot of drinking, and a little bit of brawling."

"I'll be there in two hours!"

"I'll meet you at the airport. Oh, by the way, bring a tux."

"A tux? You mean, as in tuxedo?"

"As in tuxedo."

Barney Riley was groaning as he hung up the phone.

FIVE

The hotel pool was crowded. Sexy, near-naked bodies lounged around the sides on deck chairs, air mattresses, or directly on the blue-tinted cement.

In the pool, a water polo game had started, with guys acting as horses and long-limbed, bronze-skinned girls on their shoulders, their skimpily covered breasts bouncing as they jockeyed the men.

Two bars had been set up on the lawn near the pool, along with several tables on which was spread a lavish buffet. It was only a little after eight o'clock, but already the guests—most of them—had managed to acquire a nice buzz that Carter knew would lend itself to the coming events.

Nick Carter lounged against one of the bars, sipping a nonalcoholic something that fizzed. Monroe had been able to obtain a tux for him through the hotel staff, plain black with no frills.

He looked like a weary retiree who had long ago faded into the background.

In a group of men to his left, on the far side of the pool, a raucous argument had broken out. Without turning his head, Carter recognized Barney Riley's voice above the others.

51

In less than a half hour, Riley had managed to consume great amounts of liquor and make himself generally obnoxious to about eighty percent of the guests.

He hadn't zeroed in on Komuku yet, but that was the plan . . . the plan that earlier in their suite had caused Colin MacIntyre's face to turn a chalky white.

"I won't have it! Dear God, fighting *here*, at the hotel, among the guests? And you want my security people to let it go on?"

"Right down to the last punch," Carter said, then applied a little more verbal pressure.

It had taken about a half hour, but the old Scot had finally acquiesced, thrown up his hands, and fled from the suite.

"I don't know what you think this is going to prove," Riley had said, sitting on one of the beds and sipping a whiskey.

"For sure? I don't know either, Barney. But I'm guessing that if this Komuku is the expert I think he is, he's going to give you a pasting in a very special way."

"That's a goddamned comforting thought, Nick."

Carter ordered another something that fizzed and watched out of the corner of his eye as Barney worked his way inexorably toward the group of Japanese that included Komuku.

He let his eye travel forward to the young Japanese. Komuku wore a pair of swim trunks beneath a loosely belted robe that came to his hips. He was much smaller in bulk than Barney Riley, but his body looked every bit as powerful and much more lithe as he moved through the group smiling and chatting with animation.

"Hi."

She was built as a woman was meant to be built, in a one-piece swimsuit that accentuated rather than hid every curve and hollow in her body. Her legs were unbelievably long and so perfectly shaped it seemed as if they had been sculpted. Her breasts, barely contained by the suit, thrust upward and outward magnificently.

She noticed the direction of Carter's gaze and smiled. "They have help standing alone."

"I couldn't help but wonder," Carter chuckled.

"My name's Lily. You with the convention?"

Carter almost said no, noticed something in her tone, and answered in the affirmative instead.

"You want some company?"

And then he knew. Lily was one of the pros that Monroe had brought in to comfort the single contingent of convention members. She had been one of the bareback riders in the pool. The conventiongoers who had brought their wives were all in tuxedos around the bar and food tables, staring moodily at those in the pool.

"Why me?" Carter asked. "I'm an old man." He ran his hand through his gray wig as though to emphasize his words.

"Because you look safe," she admitted. "I've had my share of the rough ones this weekend."

Carter smiled. "Sure, have a drink."

As he ordered the lady's preference from the bartender, he heard Riley's voice again raised in anger. A quick glance told him that the Irishman had reached Komuku's group, and he had zeroed in on the dapper Japanese golfer.

Carter couldn't hear all the words, but it was obvious that Riley had already gotten the man's goat. The basic thrust of the argument seemed to be the difference between fighting styles, the old rock-'em-sock-'em American way as opposed to the fancy footwork and finesse indigenous to the Far Eastern styles of the martial arts.

"Shee-it," Riley roared, "I met head-on once in L.A., in Chinatown, with one of your hot karate experts. *'Hai ka-rate!'* he says to me, wiggling his goddamned arms and flexin' his toes like you experts do. You know what I did? Well, hell, I said 'Hai chair!' and broke one over the bastard's head, that's what I did! He fell like a tiny tree and never got up!''

Komuku smiled and nodded inscrutably and tried to get away from Riley's boorishness. Riley would have none of it and pursued his prey right to the edge of the pool, needling him all the way.

''I got a hundred—hell, *five* hundred—that says I can hit you ten times before you lay a finger on me!''

Komuku held up his hands, palms out, smiled, nodded, and bowed. He said something, low, that only Riley could hear. It brought a roaring laugh from the Irishman, who lashed out at the smaller man's shoulder. The blow was glancing, but it almost knocked Komuku into the pool.

''Interesting,'' Carter said to Lily. ''An amusing sideshow. Shall we?''

The presence of the girl on his arm would add a nice cover.

''No,'' she answered quickly, drawing back.

''What?''

''I know that Japanese bastard,'' she said tightly. ''I was with him last night. He's a sadist.''

Interesting, Carter thought, and an added stroke of luck. He captured the girl's arm and, before she could protest any further, led her toward the fray.

''Ah, don't worry, my dear. You're with me now.''

She moved with him, but he could tell from her face that she wanted no part of Ishi Komuku.

The argument was heating up considerably. From shouting at each other, the two men were now speaking slowly, in low, ominous tones.

''I know that you were a prizefighter, Mr. Riley,'' Komuku said in even, modulated tones. ''I want no trouble with you.''

''Why? Because you can't handle it?'' Barney Riley bellowed. ''You just got through saying you've studied the ancient art of kumazuzu, or some such crap. Don't you believe in it?''

"I do, Mr. Riley, but you are drunk."

"Hell, I could take three of you with just my right, drunk or sober!"

"I want no trouble with you, Mr. Riley," Komuku repeated, his face becoming flushed, his body tensing.

Carter was barely able to suppress a chuckle. Barney was doing a splendid job. He only hoped the ex-prizefighter didn't get killed in the effort.

"Golfer," Riley said, pushing. "Christ, if you're such a hotshot at kakazumu—or whatever the hell you call it—how come you got to hit little white balls for a living? And I understand you got to play with *amateurs* to look good at it!"

Now Carter himself tensed. The little Oriental's face was filled with anger. Maybe Carter had overestimated him. Maybe Komuku couldn't control himself after all.

If that was the case, Riley was in real trouble.

"I understand, Mr. Riley," Komuku hissed between clenched teeth, "that you now scribble for a second-rate magazine."

"At least it's a goddamned living and I do it in my own country!" Riley roared. "I got expenses, but I don't live off other people. First I got taxes, then I got alimony—in my case for *two* wives. And the two wives each got a brat. I still don't know if they're mine or not, but I'm payin' child support on 'em. Then you gotta live on a scale high enough in this stupid business so everyone doesn't go around sayin' that you're out of work or on the skids!"

Carter could feel more tension building in his body. Riley might be going too far.

"Let's get out of here," Lily said at his side.

Carter gripped her arm tighter to his side. "Soon, my dear. This is interesting."

He wanted to keep her around. If she had spent the previous night with Komuku, she might have a very enlightening tale to tell.

Komuku was trying to sidestep his way around the larger

man. "If you'll excuse me, Mr. Riley . . ."

"Excuse you? Hah!"

Riley landed one, dead center in the other man's gut. It lifted Komuku at least two feet off the ground and deposited him in the pool.

A crowd had gathered now from around the tables, and Carter could hear bets being made on the outcome of what looked to be headed for a brawl.

The betting was about fifty-fifty, either way. Several of the people had already recognized Barney Riley and knew his background.

Carter could see security people gathering on the outskirts of the crowd, but none of them was making a move to break it up.

MacIntyre was being true to his word so far.

Komuku gathered his feet beneath him and slowly emerged from the pool. He held his hands out in front of him again, palms facing Riley.

"I repeat, I do not want to fight with you, Riley."

"Don't ye now?" Riley replied, slowly sipping from a glass of champagne he had rescued from a nearby table.

"No, I do not. This is stupid."

With the ridiculous grin on his face that he had worn throughout the entire argument, Riley leaned precariously toward the other man. Almost gently, he tossed the remainder of the champagne in the Japanese man's face.

"You are a drunken fool, Mr. Riley."

Barney Riley didn't reply, but his lips split in a wide, drunken grin. He hunched his shoulders and moved forward, bringing comments from the onlookers. Riley's shuffle was that of a trained fighter.

More bets quickly went around the crowd, with Barney now a four-to-one favorite due to the seventy-five pounds he had on Komuku, plus the indication that he was no stranger to fighting.

And the fact that he was an Irishman didn't hurt.

The Japanese was still backing away when a hard, stinging left caught him high on the right temple. There was nothing else he could do but take a stand before the bigger man.

Riley's left flicked out in exploration, and Komuku covered. It flicked again, hitting the smaller man's shoulder and jarring him. A right came from nowhere to his other shoulder with jolting force. He spun in a complete circle and barely got his balance to keep from toppling into the pool again.

Quickly, the little man backpedaled before the advancing Irishman, to re-form his defenses. "I'm telling you, Mr. Riley, I do not want a battle. I will even apologize!"

Riley bore in. Now there was no semblance of drunkenness about him. His big body moved on cat feet, and his heavy shoulders seemed to be on a well-greased axis as his hands opened and closed into fists.

"I'll have your apology, lad," Riley chuckled. "I can take smart alecks like you with my eyes closed. When I'm done makin' you good and bloody, then I'll have your apology!"

Carter checked the security men again. They looked as if they were about to succumb to apoplexy, but not a one of them moved in to break it up.

And the tipsy crowd was loving the sudden break in the boredom.

Riley's left flashed out again, so fast that Komuku failed to block it, again and yet again. Blood suddenly flowed like a river from the smaller man's nostrils, and cuts appeared on both his cheeks. The Irishman's weight was forward, on the balls of his feet. He moved with a grace that didn't fit with his massive bulk. Komuku took one blow after another.

Then, with a look of startled exasperation on his bloody face, he found himself flat on his back in a flower bed.

It was all too evident to the crowd—those that didn't already know—that Riley had been in the professional ring at one time in his life. That experience, plus the larger man's greater weight, made the whole confrontation a total mismatch.

A female voice rang out from the fringes of the crowd, saying as much. "Stay down! He's a pro. He'll cut you to pieces!"

Riley continued to dance around Komuku's prone body, taunting him. "Get up, hot shot," he growled. "We've just gotten started."

Somehow, Komuku managed to pull himself back up to his feet and assume a semblance of the boxer's stance that Riley was already using. The Irishman came in again, faster this time. He was gaining confidence, having taken the measure of his opponent and finding him lacking.

Komuku attempted to block, attempted to get a right and a left in himself, and failed. He took another stunning blow to the heart, but this time he only staggered back, keeping himself from falling.

Somebody yelled from the opposite side of the pool, "Stop it! Stop this nonsense! Riley will kill him!"

"Shut up!" someone else rumbled drunkenly. "It's a good fight."

Riley seemed to be appreciating the audience. He began operating more spectacularly. His blows became defter, more cunning, but without the power to put Komuku away. It was as if Riley were stringing the massacre out, wanting to prolong his moment of glory.

He danced to the side deftly, then moved in quickly. He threw a clever, sharp left. Komuku stumbled back. A crushing right landed smack on his mouth and he went down again, this time blacking out for the briefest of moments.

"You through?" Riley asked, dancing back a few steps. "Had enough, little man?"

All emotion, even anger, suddenly faded from the Oriental's face. It was as though an eraser had passed across the blackboard of his features, leaving them totally blank. He put his hands to the ground and came erect again. He spat blood and part of a chipped tooth and brought his hands up in front of him.

"All right, Mr. Riley," he said, his voice a flat, deadly monotone, "we shall see who gives the lesson now. Let us continue."

He slipped his body into a lay-out stance, one foot forward with toes pointing straight ahead and knees slightly bent, hands forward, knuckles up. He appeared to be almost parallel to the ground.

Riley stared at him uncomprehendingly. "What the hell is this? You gonna fight or do push-ups?"

"Let us proceed, Mr. Riley," Komuku grunted.

Riley shrugged, laughed, and came dancing forward. He still used the prizefighter's prancing steps, his hands still exhibiting the lightning quickness of a professional's moves.

But this time none of his blows landed. Komuku's body wasn't there.

A guttural growl and then a high-pitched, piercing shout erupted from the Oriental's throat as he bent his body slightly to the right in a downward motion. At the same time, he threw a left-hand block hard against Riley's wrist, locking it in the vise of his fingers. With his own left, Komuku applied a quick wristlock and began twisting Riley's arm inward and outward.

With his right hand, knuckles curved into a claw rather than a fist, he rapped the bigger man with a bone-jarring blow behind the ear.

The Irishman screamed with pain. Komuku quickly released the wrist, stepped back with his right foot, and kicked ahead with a left straightforward karate kick to Riley's midsection.

As the heavier man began to crumble, he fell forward. Komuku moved in and delivered a slashing chop with the edge of his hand across Riley's clavicle.

By the time the security men and a doctor had moved in to administer to Riley, Carter was already leading the girl, Lily, toward the privacy of the clubhouse lounge.

He had just watched Komuku execute a near perfect

Kokutsu-dachi. It was as good or better than any master could have done. Carter knew. He was a master himself.

It was the kind of master training that could be used for self-defense, as Carter had just witnessed. But it wasn't the kind of rigorous training a normal devotee of the martial arts went through for sport alone.

It was too hard, too lengthy, and too involved with the pure act of one man killing another with only his bare hands as weapons.

Carter had no doubts now as to the identity of Ward Christopher and Fancy Adams's killer.

Barney Riley groaned, opened his eyes, saw that Carter had three heads, and closed them again.

Carter put a glass in the Irishman's hand and ran a cloth across his forehead.

"How'd I do?" Riley's voice was a gravelly croak when he spoke. He tried to smooth it out with the contents of the glass and ended up choking.

"You did wonderfully," Carter replied. "If there was a doubt before, there's none now. And I also learned some interesting things from a very lovely young lady about our Mr. Ishi Komuku's kinky sexual desires."

"Bravo, terrific," Riley said, draining the glass and holding it out for a refill. "The bloody bastard almost killed me."

"Do you feel alive?"

Riley tried to nod and found that he couldn't. His neck was in a brace. He then took stock and found his left arm in a sling and his chest swathed in bandages.

"Good God, what all did the bugger do to me?"

"Snapped a collarbone, cracked two ribs, and sprained your left wrist. You're lucky he had control."

"You call that lucky?" Riley bellowed.

"Barney, if he's as good as I think he is, he could have severed your windpipe or broken your neck any time he wanted."

Riley's face went a little white. "How could you be so sure he wouldn't then, when you suggested I start our little argument?"

Carter shook his head. "He wouldn't dare, not in front of all those people. That would have prompted an inquiry, and that's exactly what he wants to avoid. All he wants now is to get out of the country as quickly and quietly as possible."

"Then you got what you wanted?"

"I sure as hell did," Carter replied, gently squeezing the other man's good arm. "And I'll make all the broken bones up to you, starting right now."

Carter moved to the door connecting the two bedrooms, opened it, and returned with the tallest, most beautiful blonde Barney Riley had ever seen.

"Her name is Lily, Barney, and she wants to meet you in the worst way."

"Is that so?" the Irishman said, his face breaking into an impish grin. "Well, just sit right down here on the bed, little darlin'."

"Golly, Mr. Riley, you were wonderful! Were you really champion of the world?"

"I sure was, darlin', twice. Almost. Aren't you warm with all those clothes on?"

"It's just a beach robe over my bikini," she replied with a shrug.

"I know. The robe looks very warm . . ."

As Carter moved out the door, the robe was dropping from Lily's shoulders. He wondered idly if Barney would be able to operate in all his braces and bandages.

It would be interesting to find out, but he had phone calls to make.

One to Milo Ferris, to bring him up-to-date and convince him not to arrest Ishi Komuku.

Another to Pan Am, to book a seat on the next day's 2:15 flight to Hong Kong.

SIX

The flight was uneventful. Komuku had reserved a first class seat. Carter, under an AXE-produced passport in the name of Silas Cavendish, importer of Oriental art, sat in the far rear smoking area of the tourist section.

As an added precaution, he had stayed far away from Komuku in the boarding area and got on the plane way ahead of him. There was little chance that Komuku would remember him from the crowd around the pool, but Carter was taking no chances.

He had given his word to Milo Ferris that the file on the Christopher/Adams killing would be closed in a week's time. He meant to keep that promise.

They landed at Kai Tak Airport on the Kowloon side of Hong Kong a little after seven in the evening. Purposely, Carter had taken only carry-on luggage so he could bypass the baggage claim area and go immediately through Customs.

A uniformed policeman waited in the open area beyond Customs. His eyes grew wide when he saw Carter. It was as if the Killmaster could see the gears in his brain going over the

Ident that had been telexed to his office from Interpol in San Francisco: six-feet-two, medium build, and slightly stooped with a limp. Appears to be just over sixty, with a lined face, and wears a mustache about the same shade of gray as his hair.

The man was about to step forward and identify himself, when Carter shook his head and moved on by him without a pause. The young officer understood and fell in behind him about five paces back.

In the outside walkway, out of sight of the baggage area, Carter slowed his pace and motioned the man forward with a nod of his head.

"Mr. Carter?"

"Yes."

"We have two cars waiting, sir, just as you requested. This way."

It was Carter's turn to fall in behind the officer. They worked their way through a mob of howling cab drivers and crossed two lighted bays. At the end of the second sat two black sedans, both occupied.

Carter was glad to see that other than the officer he followed, none of the men were in uniform.

The two Chinese in the front of the first sedan barely nodded as he passed. The officer opened the rear door of the second car, and Carter slid inside.

There was a Chinese driver and a young Caucasian in front. Half the rear seat was occupied by an older man with a thick, old-school mustache and a bull-shouldered figure with a solid head set on a neck that didn't seem to turn.

It was to him that the uniformed officer spoke after closing the door behind Carter. "Will that be all, sir?"

"Indeed, thank you, Sergeant," the man replied, then turned to the Killmaster, extending his hand. "Mr. Carter, I am Commander Julian Jarvis."

"Nick. Happy to meet you, Commander."

"As you can see, we are meeting with your requests to the

letter. The men in both cars are some of my best. We could trail him clear to the Chinese frontier without him spotting us.''

"Any line on him here in Hong Kong?''

"None, at least not under the name you have given us. We followed the golf thread you suggested and came up with nothing. Also, there is no one on the refugee lists, the foreign rolls, or the tax lists with the name Ishi Komuku.''

"I didn't think there would be,'' Carter said and sighed. "He operates out of Japan. My guess is that he has a safe house he uses here between jobs. It's probably under a phony name.''

Jarvis nodded. "Entirely possible. Nearly a quarter of the people flowing in and out of the colony do so illegally. As you know, the status of Hong Kong makes it nearly impossible to keep up with everyone. Smoke?''

Carter nodded and accepted a cigarette from the gold case in the man's hand. "He should be out shortly. He's wearing a white-on-white sport shirt, tan summer suit, and carrying two bags, one large and one carry-on, as well as a couple of golf bags.''

The last word was barely out of Carter's mouth before the driver was on the two-way radio, relaying the description to the men in the lead sedan.

Carter smiled in satisfaction as he bent his head and accepted a light from Jarvis.

These boys were good; he could sense it.

"Sounds like a good show,'' the commander said drily. "Can you sketch it for me?''

Carter met the clear, piercing intensity in the other man's eyes and inclined his head toward the front of the car.

"No fright. They both have the same clearance I do, tops. We're all overseas colonial security.''

"Does that read MI6?''

The smile was like ice, but it said worlds. "Of course.''

Carter gave him a quick, abbreviated rundown, but it was

more than enough to tell him what had occurred up to that point and what was at stake securitywise.

"Sounds big enough for a bit of fun."

"I'm sure it will be, Commander. By the way, were you able to make my hotel reservations?"

"Just as you requested, the Shangri-La, Mody Road, here on the Kowloon side. It's the best, but then I understand you chaps have wide latitude on your expense accounts."

"Only when the job is this big, Commander."

"Sir, he's coming out!"

The car hummed into life, and Carter was elated when he saw all the gears meshing without a single command. The lead sedan pulled away without being told, passed the long line of taxis, and headed for the main exit of Kai Tak Airport. Somewhere out there, they would wait to begin the tail.

Komuku climbed into a taxi, and they were off.

Within minutes they were threading their way through every imaginable kind of blaring traffic, from rickshaws and pushcarts to taxis and bicycles.

As they moved, trading places directly behind Komuku's taxi, Hong Kong and Kowloon swam through the car window, overwhelming Carter.

It had been years since he had been there, and now everything seemed to have been built up . . . *literally* up. Skyscrapers were everywhere, reaching to the sky and spreading toward the rising hills that led to the Chinese frontier.

And yet nothing had changed.

The night was still garish with neon signs, and laundry seemed to be everywhere, hanging on outside lines in hopes that it would dry before morning in the humid air. The stark laundry seemed to mesh with the gray buildings, the staircased streets, and the thousands of frenetically milling people.

And permeating it all were the smells. Almost everywhere, in any large city in the world, there is a distinctive smell.

Hong Kong island and its neighbor, Kowloon, were no different.

"Something?"

Jarvis's voice brought Carter from his reverie. He suddenly realized that he had been daydreaming.

"Nothing . . . I was just thinking about the sounds and smells. The wind is full of flowers, and the sounds it brings are of abacuses counting money."

Jarvis chuckled. "I see you have spent some time in Hong Kong."

"He's leaving the cab, sir."

The driver's voice drove into Carter's thoughts, bringing him back to the matter at hand.

"Odd bloke," Jarvis said. "He's walking away from his luggage."

"No, he isn't," Carter said. "My guess is he's given instructions to the taxi driver where to drop it off. He's being cagier than I thought he would be. But then it's a way of life for him, making sure of his anonymity."

Carter barked suggestions to Jarvis, who relayed them with a mere nod of his head. The driver, in turn, relayed to the other car ahead.

Everyone moved as one. Carter and the other Englishman exited the sedan. One of the two men in the other car also got out as his mate sped off to follow the taxi. Jarvis would stay with his driver to act as communications center for the stalkers.

"Name's Giles Gordon."

"You know mine," Carter said. "You have a two-way?"

The man opened his jacket to show Carter the two-way radio attached to his belt. "We all do."

"Good. Let's go!"

The three of them alternated behind Komuku as he meandered through the narrow streets with no obvious destination in mind. But Carter could sense that the man was setting out to lose a tail, even though the Killmaster was positive that the little Japanese had not detected the fact that he had one.

It was merely a part of the animal he was, living by a code that dictated one thing: survival.

Twice he took rickshaws, and after the last one, he jumped a streetcar. Carter took directions and orders from Gordon and his Chinese comrade. They knew the territory and could practically outguess Komuku's moves.

As Carter had guessed, Jarvis's men were good. Between himself and the other two men, their quarry was never out of sight.

The radio crackled on Gordon's belt. He put it to his ear and mumbled a reply. "He's heading deep into the old quarter, near the water."

"Any chance of losing him there?"

"There's a chance," Gordon replied, "but it's slim. My turn to take the lead. Keep your eye on my back!"

Carter did, and noticed that the Chinese officer had cut over two blocks to rush ahead and come out in front of Komuku. When he was passed, he picked up and Gordon dropped back.

Two more turns and they came up short in a nearly deserted alley. Only one neon sign was piercing the darkness between the buildings lining both its sides.

The Red Cap.

"It's a restaurant and bar."

The words were barely out of his mouth when the other officer came out the door of the Red Cap and trotted toward them.

"He's having a drink at the bar. I'm fairly sure he's ready to make his last move."

"Good," Gordon nodded. "Back exit?"

"Yes, comes out into Thieves' Alley and runs to the water. I'll take it."

He scurried away, and Gordon moved on down the alley. When he was a few yards beyond the door of the restaurant, he darted into the darkness of a doorway.

Carter lit a cigarette and moved into a niche between buildings to wait.

His eyes were heavy. The sixteen-hour flight was beginning to tell on him. He had managed to sleep a good part of the trip, but snoozing in a seated position had never been his bag for restful sleep.

He had just ground the cigarette beneath his sole when he saw Gordon moving back to his position.

"Our man has moved out. Ling is following him now. He changed clothes, probably in the men's room . . . Chinese pajamas. He's playing coolie, and moving toward the bay."

"You think he had help in the Red Cap?"

"Could be," Gordon said, "but doubtful. He probably had the clothes stashed somewhere in the loo. Ling said he's carrying a butcher paper-wrapped bundle under his arm. It's probably the suit he was wearing."

The radio crackled again. Gordon clawed it from his belt and held it between himself and Carter. "Go ahead!"

"He rowed out to a junk. It's anchored about fifty yards out in the bay. A woman met him at the ladder."

"What's your position?"

The officer, Ling, rattled it off, and they were moving.

They were almost to the water when the radio talked some more. Gordon listened, checked, and spoke to Carter as they moved.

"Your guess was right. The cabdriver dumped all his bags with a rickshaw driver."

"And . . . ?"

"And the rickshaw driver trotted right back to the airport and stowed them in a locker."

Carter smiled. "Our boy is very thorough. Evidently he plays no golf in Hong Kong."

They came out on Bay Street, Kowloon side, which was no more than a wide cement slab with buildings on one side and jutting piers on the other. Nearly every pier had a boat of some kind tied up to it. In the bay, about fifty yards out, were several dozen junks, all tied to each other in a long, unending line.

Ling met them just at the mouth of Thieves' Alley. "It's the *Tokyo Star*. That big one. If it belongs to Komuku, he's a man of means."

Carter followed the man's pointing finger. The junk was big, at least a third larger than any of those around. Lanterns waved from its bow, stern, and mast, and in their light Carter could see what Ling meant.

Junks that size, and outfitted like the *Tokyo Star*, didn't come cheap.

"All right, Carter, we've got him. Now what?"

The Killmaster did a quick recon, then returned to the two men.

"There's a call box there on that building, and one farther down, there. Can you get them tapped?"

"Within the hour."

"And I imagine that junk has a ship-to-shore aboard."

"From the antennae on the mast, I'd say so," Ling offered. "And a powerful one."

Gordon jumped in. "We can monitor it with a direction-finding unit. Shouldn't take too long to get his frequency."

"Okay," Carter said, nodding. "Other than putting a twenty-four-hour watch on him from here, with spares to follow anybody who visits him, I can't think of anything else."

"It's as good as done," Gordon said. "You look beat."

"I feel it."

"We'll take it from here."

He got back on the radio, and three minutes later Jarvis's sedan pulled up at a pier about a hundred yards away.

Carter shook both men's hands and jogged toward the car.

"Good job, Commander," he said, sliding into the rear seat. "We should have something within twenty-four hours."

He was dropped at the Shangri-La ten minutes later. It

glistened against the lights of Victoria Harbor and the lights of Hong Kong beyond like a huge black granite jewel.

"I'll stay in close touch," Carter said, stepping from the car.

"Righto. And don't worry, Carter. My boys will stay right on top of him."

"I don't doubt it for a minute, Commander. Good night."

The lobby was as imposing as the exterior, with polished white Carrara marble, Austrian crystal chandeliers, and polished brass planters everywhere.

"Your suite is ready, Mr. Cavendish, in the rear, facing Victoria Harbor and the island."

"Thank you. Could you send a boy up with the bags? I'd like to get a drink and something to eat."

"Of course, sir," the clerk said, glancing up at the clock. "They serve sandwiches in the main lounge until twelve. You'll find the elevators right around the corner there. Go to the roof, and then follow the sound of the music."

The elevator whisked him to the roof, and he stepped out into a narrow hall with thick pile carpeting. The sound of American rock tinged with Oriental strings led him to the right and into the lounge.

The Shangri-La was a plush place, and its lounge, with its breathtaking view of the harbor and Hong Kong, was no different.

But that night it looked like Saturday night at any big stateside hotel with a convention in town.

A young girl who'd had one too many moved around the room, shaking herself at any man who would take the time to watch. An old guy in a garish Hawaiian shirt and a coolie hat grabbed her a little too roughly. She yelled at him, and when he wouldn't let go, she nailed him with a roundhouse right that would have made Barney Riley proud.

Some of the men standing at the bar roared with laughter, and a gray-haired woman with a very upper-class accent said something very lower-class about the girl. Eventually, a bellboy appeared and escorted the girl away.

Carter heard her screams all the way to the elevator.

It was the waning of a typical evening in Hong Kong.

The bar was dimly lit and filled with artificial plants, a lot of bamboo, and a few small palms. There was the smell of gin and the heady odor of women's perfume, the hard rhythm of the band, and the oppressive heat of many bodies jammed together.

Carter located a table near the picture windows and sat down. A waitress stopped at a nearby booth, picked up her tip and a couple of empty glasses, then come over to him.

"My name is Soo. May I help you?"

Carter ordered a small dish of *dim sum* and a stiff double scotch.

"Will that be all?"

He might have been wrong, but he thought he saw it in her wide, almond eyes, the twist of her lips, and the way she had left the top two buttons of her uniform open.

"For now," he replied.

He knew for sure when she returned with the food and the drink, as well as a package of Cabons, a harsh Turkish cigarette.

Carter hated them, and few people didn't. That's why, when they were delivered without being ordered, it made a great means of identification.

He pocketed the cigarettes and sipped the drink. Soo leaned across the table, emptying the ashtray and giving Carter—as well as the tipsy man at the next table—a great look at her mile of cleavage.

"Care for anything else?"

"I'm in suite nine-eleven."

She nodded. "I get off in a half hour."

She moved away. As Carter attacked the meat-filled dumplings, the man at the table beside him leaned over.

"Damn, but you're a lucky chap. Every bloke in the place has been trying to get to that one all night!"

Carter shrugged. "Just one of my days, I guess."

He finished his drink, wolfed down the last of his *dim sum*, and headed for the suite.

Exactly a half hour later, there was a light rap on the door.

Carter opened it, she stepped into the room, and he closed it behind her.

Then, and only then, did he brush his lips across the cheek of Soo Lee Culpepper, agent N11, AXE Far East, Hong Kong area.

SEVEN

Soo Lee couldn't suppress a giggle as he peeled off the wig to reveal his shaved head.

"Hawk's call said to expect a different N3 from the pictures I've seen, but that's a lot more different than I dreamed it would be!" she said and laughed behind a doll-like hand.

Carter chuckled and peeled the mustache away, along with his jacket, shirt, and tie. "It's been a rough week."

"I heard. Want to bring me up-to-date first? It might fit with whatever I've already been able to dig up."

"Good enough."

She followed Carter into the bath and perched on the edge of the tub while he peeled off the rest of the makeup and removed a day's growth of beard.

As he detailed everything out and told Soo Lee about the evening's chase, he threw quick glances in her direction.

They had never worked together before, but like the other agents in the worldwide AXE network, Carter knew her background and knew she was good.

Her father had been English and her mother Chinese. The result of the marriage was beautiful.

As he saw her now, perched like a little girl on the tub, hands in her lap, her legs crossed, he wondered idly if he could combine a little pleasure with the business at hand.

She had replaced the uniform she had worn in the lounge with a stunning dress of white silk. It had a scoop bodice, with thin straps over her shoulders. The starkness of the white contrasted sharply with her deep olive-hued skin and the lustrousness of her long ebony hair.

Below the simplicity of the bodice, the skirt bunched out in a fiesta of narrow pleats like a waterfall in liquid white, with the sheerest white foam of lacy underskirts below.

By the time he finished his briefing, Carter was openly staring.

"Something wrong?"

"Not really," he replied with a lopsided smile. "I was just thinking how virginal and sweet-sixteen you look in that dress."

"It's part of the cover," she said, grinning back.

"It's a good one." He moved back into the suite and went directly to the minibar for a nightcap. It would help him sleep. "Drink?"

"God, no. After smelling the stuff for the last two nights, I couldn't stand drinking it."

"Any trouble getting a job here on such short notice?"

"None," she said. "The manager is an old friend."

"Good." Carter fell on his back across the bed, lit a cigarette, and propped himself up on the pillows. "Now, your turn."

Soo Lee took a deep breath, pulled a set of notes and what looked like photos from her purse, and began.

"Lin Duong went underground right after she heard about her brother's death."

"Any line?"

"None, and I've got ears all over the city. There is a chance, though, and you can follow it up more easily than I."

"What's that?"

"Her roommate. The girl's name is Mimi; she's French. She and Lin Duong knew each other in Saigon. Mimi works in a place called the Asian Slipper. It's a brothel in Po Alley, just off George V Boulevard."

"Did Lin work there?"

"No. Evidently Billy Duong sent her enough money to live on. She kept busy with part-time jobs for the government as a secretary."

"But she stayed friends with a prostitute?"

Soo Lee smiled. "Friendships of this kind are very strong in the Orient, Nick—you should know that."

"*Touché*," he replied. "I do. Go on."

"It's better than even money that Lin and Mimi are still in touch. Your boy, Komuku, might even be going after her if he knows of her existence."

"My guess is he doesn't. What about Connie Chu?"

"Now there's a real winner," Soo Lee said. "She owns twenty junks, and does one hell of a lot of trading everywhere, from Singapore to Taiwan. There's also a hands-off policy on her so she can trade with the Communist mainland."

"Does she do any smuggling?"

"For the record, no. But no one who owns boats from here to Macao doesn't smuggle something. It's an unwritten law. In any event, Connie Chu is a very wealthy lady, and getting wealthier."

She selected a photo from her pile and passed it to Carter.

"What's this?"

"Her little shack on the mountain at the top of Kowloon Road. It's the white one . . . the biggest."

The photo had been taken from far below with a wide-angle lens. It showed the rolling hills north to the frontier dotted with small shrines, heavy greenery, and several pala-tial villas.

One villa, its walls more massive, its tiled and slanted roof more dominating, stood out among all the others. Even its positioning, clinging to the very top of an almost inaccessible peak, made it more imposing than its neighbors.

Carter flipped the photo and jammed a finger at it. "Hers?"

Soo Lee nodded. "Beautiful, isn't it? And built like a fortress. Between the outside walls and the villa itself, there are an awful lot of armed guards and dogs."

"Then the lady has a lot of enemies?"

The woman laughed aloud. "Everyone in Hong Kong with a lot of money has enemies."

Carter knew that one reason Soo Lee functioned so well in the area was her knowledge of—and friendship with—the underbelly of the colony.

"What do they say on the street and in the bay about her?"

"That she's a rich Chinese whore from Saigon, but little else. The people who work for her are tight-knit and closemouthed. She pays them well."

"Could she still have a connection with Charlie Loo?"

"She could," Soo Lee said. "But then she could have a connection with the New York Mafia families. If anybody knows, nobody says."

"Okay. What are the other two photos?"

"A picture of Mimi, and one of Lin Duong."

Carter glanced at them and slipped them into his wallet. "Two things."

"Shoot."

"Find out what you can about a junk called the *Tokyo Star*. Not just the stuff MI6 will come up with, the *real* stuff."

"I'll try."

"And see if you can find a chink in Connie Chu's personnel. They can't all be that loyal."

"There is one captain . . . a Swede named Johannson. It's only a rumor, but I'll work on it."

"Do," Carter said and suppressed a yawn.

"You look beat."

"I am."

"Then you don't want company," she said, her lips parting to reveal the whitest teeth Carter had ever seen.

He had thought he had seen that glint in her eye when she had been sitting on the edge of the tub. He knew it had been in his look when she caught him staring so intently at her.

But it had been a long, long day.

"I do, but I'm afraid it would be a worthless try," he replied, matching her smile.

"Maybe you'll be in Hong Kong long enough," she said, brushing her lips across his and moving to the door.

"Call me in the morning?"

"I will."

The door closed behind her, and Carter was barely able to tug his pants from his legs before he fell back across the bed in a deep sleep.

Carter awoke at nine the next morning to a jangling phone and a jet-lag hangover. For some odd reason, he also had a fuzzy image of Soo Lee Culpepper, nude, on the back of his eyelids.

It was her voice on the phone. "Did you have a good night's sleep?"

"Horrible. I dreamed of you naked all night, and what I probably turned down."

"I get off at midnight tonight again," she said, a smile in her voice.

"Let's hope I'm here, and awake. Got anything?"

"Only what the British boys probably already have. The *Tokyo Star* is owned by Chansung Import-Export, Limited, of Macao. What's interesting is that they are owned in turn by Kulo Electronics."

"*Very* interesting. Anything else?"

"Captain Johannson will be finishing a run from Taiwan around three this afternoon. I'm going to be at the docks to lure him."

"Be careful."

"Will do."

Carter dropped the phone and immediately went out cold again.

At noon he forced himself awake. He ordered breakfast from room service, was told he could only have lunch, and shouted until they agreed to send breakfast for an additional charge.

In the bath, he showered, shaved again, and reapplied his makeup, wig, and mustache.

By two o'clock he felt rejuvenated and called the number that Commander Jarvis had given him the previous evening. He was put right through.

"Anything on Komuku, Commander?"

"Not as yet. He hasn't even fired up his radio, and the only visitors to the junk have been traders . . . fresh vegetables, fish, and some such. But the woman came ashore once this morning and made a call, though."

"You got it?"

"Every word, on tape, although I don't think it's anything you'd be interested in. She called a medical clinic about picking up her prescription for a female problem."

"I'll stay in touch."

"Righto."

Carter killed the afternoon by renting a car and scouting the area around Connie Chu's villa. He was saving her for last in this little game, so he was very careful not to draw attention to himself.

At teatime, he returned to the hotel. There was a call from Jarvis.

"Another call, and this one is interesting."

"I'll be right there."

Jarvis's headquarters were on the Hong Kong side. Carter took the Star Ferry and walked the few remaining blocks to the small whitewashed building that bore only a tiny plaque beside the door to tell a visitor of its official capacity.

Giles Gordon was waiting, and ushered him into Jarvis's office.

"Tea?" the old commander asked.

"No, thank you," Carter replied, "I just did."

"Good enough, then. Let's get to it. Giles?"

Gordon moved to a tape console in the wall and began pushing buttons. Carter took a chair and lit a cigarette.

"This was made about an hour ago," Jarvis said, "from one of the call boxes along the piers."

And then a very familiar voice filled the room.

"Okamoto will be arriving tomorrow with a new shipment. He will deliver the usual way. I do not want him to return to Tokyo. It is obvious that he has been compromised."

Carter came up, tense, in his chair. "That's Charlie Loo. I'd recognize the voice anywhere!"

Jarvis raised his hand, and then Komuku came on.

"It will be taken care of."

"Also, for safety, I think the files should be moved, just in case. They are the real power we have."

"Of course," Komuku replied.

"How long will it take you to secure a new place?"

There was a pause, and when Komuku replied there was a great deal of tension in his voice. "That is difficult to say. We have moved them four times in the last six months."

"I know that, but dammit, it must be done! Without them we have no means of securing the information we sell to our Russian friends. The files must not be jeopardized!"

"I will do what I can."

"Excellent. And by the way, congratulations on the Carter affair. Very well done!"

"Thank you."

"And I may have already found a new convert at Kulo to replace Okamoto. Our people are working on compromising him now. If a file is put together, I will inform you and send it along by the usual means.''

There was a crackle of static that partially blurred the good-byes of the two men, and then the tape fell silent.

"I hope that all means more to you than it does to us," Jarvis said.

"It might . . . I hope," Carter replied. "I think I'll have that tea now."

He paced and mused while Giles Gordon prepared three cups in the English style, thick with cream, and then resumed his seat.

"We think the blackmail victims are in top positions in several Japanese computer and electronics firms. From the amount of information that has been passed, there are probably several of them."

Gordon jumped in. "So the blackmail files are here, in Hong Kong?"

"I'd say so, from what Charlie Loo said on that tape. It sounds as though Ashami Okamoto is a courier as well as a source of information. Can you find out where he stays, who he visits, what he does while he's in Hong Kong? My guess is the visits are frequent."

"Should be fairly simple," Jarvis said.

"From the sound of it," Carter murmured, "the blackmail data, as well as the pirated electronics and computer info, is gathered in Japan by Charlie Loo. Then it's carried to Hong Kong. The blackmail stuff is in a master file here, and somehow the salable info is passed to the Russians here."

"So what's our next move?"

"For you and your people, Commander, I'd say stay on Ishi Komuku like glue. He seems to be more than just a hired killer."

"Quite," Jarvis agreed. "Sounds as though he runs this end."

"Maybe," Carter growled. "Let's just hope we can get a line on those files from him. Meanwhile, I'm going to see if I can find Billy Duong's sister. There's a good chance Billy told her a hell of a lot more than we think he did.''

Carter took a taxi to the harbor end of George V Boulevard and walked back. The entrance to Po Alley was so narrow, and the sign marking it so obscure, that he almost missed it.

Number 12 was a quiet-looking three-story house in a section that had once been totally colonial. It retained some of its bygone charm, being set back from the alley and guarded by a low fence.

He moved through the gate and up a flagstone walk. The door sported an old pull bell with a white porcelain handle. He pulled it and waited.

He'd expected a woman. The little old man who answered the door looked like Fu Manchu's uncle who had been hooked up to an opium pipe just a little too long.

"Yes?''

"I was told a gentleman could spend a few entertaining hours beneath your roof.''

The door opened, and Carter was motioned in. Inside was an anteroom as dark as an underground cavern.

"This way,'' the old man mumbled and shuffled toward a slice of light.

Carter followed him into what looked like an old-fashioned drawing room, except that there was a bar and a few tables. The men who sat at them were both Chinese and Caucasian. They all looked like prosperous businessmen on a tea break.

"You wait here,'' the old man said. "You have drink if you want.''

Carter ordered a double scotch from the barman, a young lad with huge glasses who looked like a student. The drink spread a relaxing warmth through his body as he eyeballed his fellow customers. None of them even glanced back at him.

"I am Madame Wong. May I be of service?"

Even by Chinese standards she was matronly, with a kind, round face and her black hair pulled back severely from her wrinkled features.

"I was told you have very lovely ladies and that your house is very discreet."

"I see. Do you have identification? We have very strange laws here in Hong Kong."

Carter passed her the Silas Cavendish passport and an international driver's license in the same alias.

She examined the documents, passed them back, and smiled sweetly. "We have to be careful, you know, especially with new customers."

"I understand. There was a girl recommended to me . . . Mimi?"

"Ah, yes, very lovely and very popular. She is French, you know. You have traveler's checks or cash?"

"Cash."

The smile broadened. "Mimi is in room six, right up those stairs. I will tell her she has a caller. You may go up whenever you are ready. Just leave your donation on the tray at the foot of the stairs."

Carter nodded and she moved away.

Donation, he thought. *How interesting*. It was a class place, no mention of the amount. Of course, if the "donation" was too small, he was sure there would be an added one suggested before the upstairs festivities began.

He finished his drink and headed for the stairs. At the tray he was very generous, then he found number six with no trouble.

The door was ajar, so he just walked in.

"Oh, you surprised me!"

She was standing at a vanity, dressed—or undressed—in the filmiest nightie Carter had ever seen. Her small breasts gleamed white through the material, and the dark nipples caused pleats in the cloth where they pushed it away from the rest of her body.

"Sorry, the door was ajar."

"It's all right," she said and smiled. "I am Mimi. We will have great fun together, yes?" Her face had a saucy, impish look, with dark eyes, a tiny nose, and bright red lips.

"Yes, great fun."

Carter closed the door and did a quick perusal of the room. It wasn't bare, but it sported no more than the necessities. He doubted if there was a bug.

She came over to him, still smiling, and took both his hands in hers. She was short but stood very erect. When she raised to her toes, the gown parted to reveal her breasts.

Carter looked, and then looked away.

"You are bashful," she giggled in a charming, high-pitched tone. "Don't worry, Mimi will take care of that."

She started with his tie, but Carter stopped her hands.

"Not bashful, Mimi, I want to talk with you."

"Talk? Ah, you must be an American! Very well, we talk first."

She perched on the side of the bed and cocked her head to the side as if she were a small bird. Carter pulled a chair over and sat on its edge. His knees were almost touching her as he took her hands and held them.

"Mimi, I am an American. I work for the government."

"Many gentlemen in government visit Mimi," she said.

"I'm looking for Lin Duong."

Her face and body went to stone.

She squirmed like a little cat to get away, but Carter held her hands in the vise of his.

"I know Lin may be in trouble," he whispered.

"I know nothing! Let me go, please!"

"I am a friend of Billy Duong, a close friend. I'm the man Billy was trying to contact in the United States."

The struggling stopped, but the eyes still flashed like those of a hunted animal.

"How do I know this is true?"

"I can't really prove it to you, but you must believe me. I think Billy may have told his sister a great deal about the trouble he is in. He may have also mentioned me to Lin. I must talk to her."

"I do not know where she is. Let me go!"

Carter took a chance and released her. For a second he thought she would bolt for the door, but instead she wrapped her arms tightly around herself and began to pace.

"You are with the American government?"

"Yes."

"How would she know you?"

"She wouldn't remember me in person. She was very young when we met in Saigon. But she would know my real name."

"And what is that?"

Carter hesitated. If this was a dead end and Mimi knew of Komuku, things could get sticky. He didn't want the little Japanese assassin to know he was still alive . . . at least, not yet.

"You are cautious," she said, her tone one of accusation as she stopped directly in front of him.

"Yes, I admit that I am," Carter said. "There are certain people in Hong Kong that I don't want to know I am here."

She seemed to weigh this, shrugged, and then returned to the bed. "I think I must trust you. Before Lin left, she said that someone might come from America."

"Left? She's not in Hong Kong?"

"I do not know. But there is a woman, a friend to both of us, who does know where she is."

"Can you have this woman get in touch with me?"

"I can."

"I am at the Shangri-La, suite nine-eleven. I am registered under the name of Silas Cavendish. Can you remember that?"

"I can," Mimi said evenly, not taking her eyes from Carter's. "What is the real name Lin would recognize?"

Carter returned her stare. "I think you would be safer, Mimi, if you didn't know."

The eyes narrowed, and now the small dark pupils were filled with fear. "I will contact this woman."

Carter nodded and brushed her forehead with his lips. "You won't regret it."

He took his wallet from inside his jacket pocket and from it removed a thick wad of bills.

"What is this for? You have paid downstairs."

"This has nothing to do with this place or your business. This is money for you to get out of Hong Kong. Once you have contacted the woman, and you are sure she will meet me, I want you to leave until it is safe. Do you have a place you can go?"

"I do."

"Good." He checked his watch. "Has it been long enough so they won't suspect anything if I leave?"

"Yes," she said, forcing a chuckle. "Some men only take five minutes."

Madame Wong met him at the bottom of the steps. "You have enjoyed your visit with Mimi?"

"Very much so," Carter replied. "I shall recommend your house to all my business associates."

"Thank you so much," she smiled, executing a low bow as he moved through the door.

In the street, he grabbed a taxi and returned to the Shangri-La. There were no messages at the desk, and the red light wasn't lit on the phone in his room.

He ordered dinner from room service and ate staring at the phone.

It was nearly an hour until it rang.

"Yes?"

"Is this Silas Cavendish?"

"Yes, Mimi, it's me."

"I talked to the lady. She refused to meet you."

"Damn."

"But I am convinced you should. I am going to give you her name and number. I have a flight to Singapore in one hour. Please don't call until my flight leaves."

"You have my word on it."

"It's Mrs. Bruno Falkner, and the number is 888-451."

"Good-bye, and thank you, Mimi."

"Good-bye, whoever you are."

He worked his way through two more cigarettes and another cup of coffee. A call to Commander Jarvis's office for an update on Komuku used up another fifteen minutes.

Billy Duong's killer hadn't made a move, not even a rumble on the phone.

He used up another twenty minutes pacing and then called the airport just to make sure the Singapore flight was in the air.

It was. He hung up and dialed the number Mimi had given him.

"Dr. Falkner's residence."

"Mrs. Falkner?"

"No, I am maid. You want speak to Mrs. Falkner?"

"Yes, please."

An agitated two minutes passed before a cool, perfectly modulated voice with a slight German accent came on the line. "This is Mrs. Falkner."

"Mimi gave me your number. Don't hang up."

"What do you want?" The voice became icy.

"To talk to you about Lin Duong."

"I've never heard of any such person."

"We have a saying in America, Mrs. Falkner . . . bullshit."

"Now I know I don't want to talk to you!"

Carter knew he was losing her, fast. He decided to go all the way. "If you can contact Lin Duong, do it, and tell her Carter is in town."

"I don't understand."

"Maybe not, but I hope she will. I'm in suite nine-eleven at the Shangri-La. Don't forget, tell her *Carter* is in town!"

He didn't give her a chance to object. He hung up.

The phone rang again in twenty minutes.

"Yes?"

"There is a shipboard restaurant. It sails the harbor. Soo Chow's. Any water taxi will know where it is."

"When?"

"An hour. I'll meet you in the lounge."

The line went dead, and Carter reached for his jacket.

EIGHT

Soo Chow's was indeed a restaurant, converted from a huge junk. The water taxi driver explained that it sailed the same route every evening around Victoria Harbor, so it was easy to find.

Other than the uniqueness of being on the water, it was like any other eatery around the world.

Carter came aboard and bypassed the dining room for the lounge located in the bow.

There was a steam table, booths or tables for waiter service, stools at a small counter near the steam table, and a long bar where two men in white jackets mixed drinks, poured wine, and uncapped beer bottles.

Carter found an empty booth and ordered a drink. Before it arrived, Mrs. Falkner slid into the booth.

She was close to thirty, with very blond hair and a model-slim figure. Her hip bones were angular and far apart in a tight Chinese dress. The dress, instead of the traditional high collar, had a scoop neck that fell forward when she did.

"My name is Pat, instead of Patrice, and you are Nicholas."

"Nick. How did you know what I looked like?"

"What do you mean?"

"You made a beeline for this booth as soon as you walked in. You obviously knew what I looked like. Otherwise, why didn't you try the booth farther down? There's a man there all by himself. And there's another . . ."

"Mimi told me. Satisfied?"

"Satisfied."

"Good. Now, do you have some identification that proves who you are?"

Carter didn't bother with the Silas Cavendish papers. He passed over the real thing.

She took one look, sighed, and fell apart. "Thank God."

"I take it you're satisfied?"

"Very. Lin told me what to look for when I met you."

"Is she safe?"

"Yes, but I think, Mr. Carter, I can tell you everything you want to know. You see, most of the information Billy Duong got was from me."

"I don't get it. What was your relationship to Billy? And how do you fit in with Lin?"

Patrice Falkner stared at her fingers nervously as she rubbed them together, then looked up. "Lin and I have been lovers for nearly two years."

Carter managed to hide the shock and lit a cigarette. "Something tells me we should be talking in a more private place."

"You're right. Come along. I have a private bungalow up in the hills."

"Is that where Lin is?"

"Yes."

Carter dropped some bills on the table and followed her, his eyes doing a number on the way her perfect derrière came alive in the sheath.

Pat Falkner.

Lin Duong.

Lovers.

Shame, Carter thought, *a damned shame*.

Pat Falkner drove. Above Kowloon, the roads got narrower. Far off to his left, Carter could see the rambling white villa that belonged to Connie Chu.

That's a twist, he thought as the car slid through a gate and came to a halt in a carport hidden from the street.

"This is it," Pat said. "My husband would die if he knew I had purchased it with his ill-gotten gains, and he would probably kill me if he knew what I used it for."

Carter didn't reply as she unlocked the door and they walked into the huge, high-ceilinged room. The one room was most of the bungalow, with a small kitchen off one end and a bedroom and bath off the other.

The woman moved to the door of the bedroom. Beyond it, Carter could hear a shower running.

"Lin . . .?"

"Yes," came the soggy reply.

"We're here."

"I'll be right out."

Pat Falkner turned to Carter. "Would you like a drink?"

"Scotch would be fine. About two fingers and a single cube."

The sound of water stopped about the time Pat handed him the whiskey. A moment later, the clean smell of scented soap filled the room, closely followed by Lin Duong in a long mandarin robe that covered her from neck to ankle. Her damp hair was brushed back over her ears in short waves, and her thin face was devoid of makeup, leaving the natural color of her cheeks and lips looking weary but youthful.

Carter thought she looked fresh and clean and not the least bit sexy.

She paused in the doorway, her eyes wide with shock as she scanned Carter's face. He could see that the age he portrayed wasn't jiving with what she knew.

"Appearances are deceiving, Lin. It's false hair and wrinkles."

She relaxed somewhat, but her eyes were still wary.

"Let's sit," Pat Falkner exclaimed. "We all look like we're standing around at a cocktail party."

They sat, and Lin was the first to speak. "You were there when it happened, Mr. Carter?" Her voice was as youthful and frail as the rest of her.

"No, I got there too late."

"But you saw him?"

Carter decided not to pull any punches. "Yes, Lin, I saw him . . . dead. It wasn't a pretty sight."

The girl was stoic; she only nodded. Pat Falkner leaned her face into her hands.

"It was my fault!"

"How is that, Mrs. Falkner?"

"I was the one, through my husband, who got Billy the job."

"I see," Carter murmured. "Suppose you start at the beginning."

Bruno Falkner met and married Patrice fresh out of medical school in Germany. He came up quickly, too quickly, in a private practice in Munich. His sideline had been illegal drugs, though she hadn't known it at the time.

They emigrated to England just ahead of the law. But, by this time, Falkner was used to the money, and the authorities were watching him. It was on to Tokyo and a teaching position. Eventually he secured a small practice on the side as a company physician to a huge electronics company.

"Was it Kulo Electronics?" Carter asked.

"It was," the woman replied. "I acted as his nurse. It was then that I learned the real source of our wealth. He was funneling raw opium from Bangkok through Tokyo to the United States."

Carter nodded. The rest of it he could guess. She confirmed it when she started to speak again.

Someone at Kulo—she thought it was one of the top executives—discovered what was going on. But instead of turning Falkner in, they made a deal with him.

"Blackmail?"

"Yes. We would move to Hong Kong, set up a clinic here, and be one link in a chain that would smuggle material from Japan through Hong Kong to God-knows-where."

"You didn't know what the material was?"

"No, not then."

"Go on," Carter urged.

The woman sighed. "My marriage has always been lousy. And, of course, there was always my . . . tendencies. I met Lin, and . . ."

Lin Duong reached over and squeezed the woman's hand. The two exchanged looks, and Billy Duong's little sister picked up the narrative.

Billy Duong was on the run. He needed a new identity and a way to go legit. Because of his computer background, Pat Falkner thought she could get him a job with her husband's old employer.

It was easy. The rub was that Duong was good. He rose in the company until he was transferred to Japan and eventually was privy to top-secret information. It was then that they pounced, using his phony papers as a lever for blackmail. Only Duong would have no part of it.

"He got in touch with me," Lin said, "and told me that the man who hired him, Ashami Okamoto, was also being blackmailed. Okamoto would make duplicate programs of everything Kulo Electronics was working on. Also, he received information from high-level employers in other electronics firms. When a great deal of information had been accumulated, Okamoto would make a business trip to Hong Kong. Kulo has many subsidiaries here."

"Then," Pat Falkner said, chiming in, "the information was passed to my husband. Billy wanted us to find out where it went from there."

"And you did?"

Lin nodded. "Right after each of Okamoto's visits, a young woman would arrive at the clinic. Pat happened to notice that the prescriptions she picked up were never recorded in the office ledgers."

"I checked once before they were passed to the woman. The pill containers were full of microfilm. Lin followed the woman—"

"And," Carter interrupted, the pieces now falling rapidly into place, "she went to a junk in the harbor called the *Tokyo Star*."

Lin nodded. "Yes, and soon after that, I found out that she is a maid in the house of Connie Chu."

Carter sighed and mashed out his cigarette. He could pretty well guess the last link in the delivery chain. One of Connie Chu's junks met a Russian trawler or submarine at sea, and passed the microfilm over to be relayed to Moscow.

Idly, he wondered how Soo Lee was doing with Captain Johannson.

"You've done quite a bit already," he said. "Can you do more?"

The two women exchanged glances again, and then Pat Falkner spoke. "I have been able to obtain false passports and identification papers for Lin and myself through underground channels. The same ones that Billy used. But we can never run until the man in Japan is in jail or dead."

"We don't know who he is," Lin said, "but he is very powerful and has many friends. Dr. Falkner once tried to get away, and this man found him within days. He barely escaped with his life."

"I know who that man is," Carter growled, "and I think I can get him. But before I move, I must get my hands on two things."

"Yes?"

"I need the identities of the men being blackmailed, and the file on them."

"I doubt if my husband knows where they are," Pat said. "I don't think he even knows where the microfilm goes after it leaves the clinic."

"Perhaps not. But then he might know without even realizing that he knows. Do you have keys to the clinic?" Pat Falkner nodded. "Good. Here is what I want you to do."

For the next twenty minutes, Carter ran through what to look for in the clinic's files. When he was finished, he stood and stretched.

"I'll stay in touch with Lin here. There is a phone?"

Lin nodded and reeled off the number. Carter repeated it back twice and then moved toward the door. "I'll walk down the hill and catch a taxi. I think it's wise from now on that I'm not seen riding around in your car."

They escorted him to the door. Just before he stepped out into the night, they kissed him on the cheeks.

It gave him a weird feeling as he moved down the hill.

Back at the hotel, he checked the rooftop lounge. Soo Lee Culpepper had not come to work that evening.

In his room he found the red light blinking on the phone.

"This is Cavendish, nine-eleven. Do I have a message?"

"Yes, sir. I will send it right up."

Carter ordered a light dinner to save the bellman two trips and stripped for a shower.

A sealed envelope and a tray of food awaited him when he emerged. The message was from Soo Lee.

It looks like a go. Captain J. doesn't mind shady work, but hates those people behind the Curtain. Will try and make our date at the same time tonight. S.L.

He ate in front of the tall window overlooking the harbor and rethought the next move.

If Johannson could be swayed, it would make matters easier. If not, a more frontal attack would be called for, and that only if Patrice Falkner could come up with the right information.

And no matter how or when the files were secured, Carter knew that eventually he would have to face Connie Chu. He didn't know for sure, but he guessed that the only way to get to and take Charlie Loo would be through her.

He checked in with Jarvis and got Giles Gordon. There was only a minor report, two visitors to the *Tokyo Star* by water taxi. One sounded like Soo Lee's captain. The other was a noted underworld character in Hong Kong named Kim See Long.

"We've put a tail on both of them, but I doubt that anything will come of it."

Carter told Gordon about the connection with Bruno Falkner's clinic.

"Doubt that we can get a tap on the phones very quickly, old chap, but we can watch the good doctor."

"No," Carter replied. "At this point that might be too dangerous. Just put someone on the clinic. That should do it for now."

Gordon rang off and Carter yawned, stripping to his shorts. With a last look at the blinking lights of Hong Kong, he stretched across the bed for an hour's rest before the hopeful arrival of Soo Lee.

When the rap came on the door, he was instantly awake and sliding off the bed almost directly into his pants.

"Yes . . . ?"

"It's me."

He cracked the door, and closed it the second she slipped through. He could tell from the excited glint in her eyes that she had a lot to tell him.

"You're bubbling."

"I know," she said. "I met Johannson in a seaman's bar in the old quarter. We fenced for about an hour, and then I decided to dump everything on the table. You should have seen his face!"

"I think I can guess. Smuggling is one thing; a Communist conspiracy is another."

"Right, and I think he can give us the jackpot!"

"How so?"

"He got a summons early this evening from Komuku. I met Johannson right after."

"And . . . ?"

"And tomorrow morning he's sailing the *Tokyo Star* to Macao. They are picking up some crates that were delivered there about three weeks ago."

"The files!" Carter hissed.

"It sounds like it. He's moved these crates several times in the past, always aboard the *Tokyo Star*. He knows they're valuable, because Komuku always brings aboard several hired guards when they move them."

"And chances are that Komuku plans on bringing them back here, to Hong Kong, for safekeeping."

"That's what Johannson thinks."

"How do we handle it? Does Johannson want money?"

Soo Lee's head shook from side to side and her crimson lips split in a wide smile. "He has money. He wants his international ticket renewed. He lost it four years ago for smuggling."

Carter sighed. "That may be tough. There's no guarantee he won't smuggle again."

"Absolutely none. In fact, he told me he probably would. But he did say that he wouldn't do it again for Connie Chu."

"Okay, I'll see what I can do. And if I *can* do it, what then?"

"You take the morning hydrofoil to Macao. It's about an hour-and-a-half ride. Check into the Estoril. Tomorrow evening, go to the casino. Johannson will contact you there. If you have his ticket and the other papers in order, he will tell you how we can take the junk."

"We?"

Soo Lee nodded. "I will be aboard. I'm joining his crew aboard the *Tokyo Star* in the morning for the run to Macao."

"You're crazy."

"Why?" she asked, her voice harsh, her face a mask of determination.

Carter couldn't think of a good, quick answer, and she saw it.

"However you plan on taking the junk, it will be much better if you have an ally on board."

"But a woman? How will Komuku accept—?"

"Nick, please," she cut in. "Over half the crews of every junk in Hong Kong Harbor are women. In Asia, we work alongside the men . . . *everyone* works, no matter the task."

He knew she was right and said so. "Okay, it's a deal. Let me see what I can come up with."

He moved to the phone and dialed Jarvis's office. Gordon came on again, and after a little arguing, he gave Carter the commander's private home number.

Jarvis himself answered and wasn't very happy about it. He sounded as if he had been awakened from a sound sleep.

"Sorry, Commander, a necessary evil," Carter said.

"Evil, old chap, is exactly the word for it. Well, what is so damnably important?"

Carter told him, briskly and to the point, leaving out the details of an actual raid on the junk. There were certain things about the method Carter planned to use that might prompt Jarvis into thinking that the American was planning on creating a major international incident.

It was better that the MI6 man learned of it *after* the fact, particularly if that did happen.

"Good God, man, this is very sticky!"

"I realize that, Commander," Carter replied in the smoothest voice he could muster. "But I think the rewards—to *both* our countries—could very well overshadow the possible consequences of what Johannson may do later.''

''But dammit, man, if his master's ticket has been revoked—and less than five years ago, at that—it would take a Queen's Mariners Board, as well as Lloyds's representatives, to reinstate it!''

''Would it, Commander? . . . If the right pressure were applied?''

''Well, there have been cases—very rare, mind you—but they have been known to stretch the law when our people were involved. Just what do you prepare to gain, may I ask?''

''If I'm lucky, the files that Charlie Loo mentioned to Komuku. This may be the break we need.''

It took another ten minutes of calm persuasion, but Carter finally got Jarvis's assurance that he would move heaven, earth, and the Mariners Board of Hong Kong to get it done.

''You won't regret it, Commander.''

''Lord, I hope not.''

''And by the way, I'll need a Portuguese visa for Macao. I'll pick them up in the morning at your office.''

There was a lot more sputtering, but Carter had worn him down. Less than a minute later he was able to extricate himself from the conversation.

He turned, elated, to an empty room. Only then did he hear the shower in the bath running.

He smiled. *Déjà vu*, he thought, remembering the scene earlier in Pat Falkner's bungalow when Lin Duong had emerged from a shower.

He lit a cigarette and waited. He heard the shower stop and the door open. Slowly, he mashed out the cigarette as he heard the rustle of a towel over Soo Lee's bare skin.

And then she emerged, his robe belted loosely around her. She paused for only a second in the doorway, then moved into the curve of his arms.

''Well?''

"We're set."

At close quarters, the bloom of her freshly scrubbed complexion was a rare and lovely thing. Her oval face with the dark almond eyes just missed real beauty, but it was nonetheless exciting and striking.

"What will you need in order to take the junk?" she asked in a husky voice. "Armswise, I mean."

"Can't we talk about that later?"

"You're right," she murmured. "I'd rather."

His fingers came up to frame her face, and his eyes noted her long dark lashes and the casual way her black hair was drawn back from her forehead. It was glossy hair, wavy but not curly, with just a few loose strands curling down and tickling her shoulders.

As he pressed his mouth to hers, her tongue slid between his lips, and somehow the robe parted. The kiss was electrifying, but not nearly as much as the heated softness of her breasts pressing eagerly against his chest.

His hands slid beneath the robe, dislodged it from her shoulders, and then went to her back.

Finally, reluctantly, he lifted his face from hers. She stood on tiptoe, her breasts still thrusting against him, her head tilted slightly to one side with her lips parted in a smile of pure sensuality.

"Bed?" he whispered.

"Bed."

They moved as one, with Carter somehow managing to divest himself of his pants and shorts.

He didn't know why, but instead of pulling her roughly into his arms and ravishing her, as he thought he wanted to, he pushed her gently back until they were lying side by side.

Soo Lee looked up at him, her eyes clear. The fine lines of her face seemed to leap out at him. The smell of her body filled his nostrils with heady perfume, the perfume of her sex. It made him want to gently wrap his arms around the woman before him and bury himself in her body.

Their lips met, only slightly parted in a kiss that spoke of tenderness and longing rather than unbridled passion. It was a long, tender kiss, and when it was over their arms slid around each other and they embraced.

"Why?" he asked simply.

"It's easier, safer, with someone in the business."

"Yeah, I know what you mean."

"And besides," she chuckled, running the tip of her tongue along his ear, "you're a legend. What red-blooded girl wouldn't want to do it at least once with a legend?"

"Shut up!"

He put his hand over her mouth as he started gently moving his hips back and forth, their bodies meeting. He looked down at her. Her hair was highlighted where it cascaded outward from her face in waves on the pillow. Her eyes were closed.

Her hands roamed over her own body, stopping now and then to knead and bring an excited flush to her skin. She cupped a breast, squeezing it outward toward his chest and further accentuating its firmness.

One of her legs was thrown slightly over the other, as if she were protecting herself. Her gleaming olive thighs merged together, framing the triangle between them and inciting his lust even more.

"I want you," he rasped. "Now!"

"Yes . . . yes," she sighed.

With her nails digging into his straining back, she drew him up over her writhing form. Carter settled between her thighs and, with a low groan, entered her.

It was like walking on air and being on fire and stretching after a good dream and being born and dying and many other things he could not think of at the moment.

All he could think of was the soft cushion of her breasts under him, the sea of her body tossing him, urging him, encompassing him. She said no words, but with her body she told him everything. And he responded.

"Soon, so soon!" she suddenly cried out, her body arching, pummeling his.

Carter moaned aloud at the sensation that followed her throaty warning. He closed his eyes and let his hands wander over her body of their own accord as the waves of delight swept through him. She shuddered violently as her head rolled from side to side on the pillow. The magical artistry of her lovemaking destroyed his touch with reality, and he felt himself caught up in a vortex of sheer sensation.

He tensed, clarity returning for one flashing instant. He croaked her name and his hands implored her roughly. The explosion followed swiftly, and it was violent and shattering. He felt himself trembling as he descended from the heights, and he heard her soothing whispers as she withdrew from him. He drifted into a timeless inertia and floated weightlessly.

"Nick?"

He stirred, lifting his lashes, unable to determine how long he had been asleep. She was standing at the foot of the bed, her body fully clothed, her hair neatly brushed, her face freshly made up.

He stretched and discovered that she had covered his body with a sheet.

"Sorry I fell asleep."

Soo Lee smiled. "You deserved some rest. You earned it."

Then she was all business again, running through the arms available. Carter told her what he would need.

"They'll be waiting for you on the hydrofoil with the purser."

"Are you leaving now?"

"I must," she nodded and broadened her smile even more, "even though I really don't want to. There is a lot to accomplish before morning."

She moved to the door, opened it, and checked the hall. Just before closing it behind her, she pursed her lips in a kiss. "See you in Macao."

Carter smiled. "In Macao."

NINE

Carter stepped from the gangway, silently thankful for the invention of the hydrofoil. It had been a swift, pleasant glide over calm waters from Victoria to the oldest European settlement in the Far East, Macao.

He fell into the long line of people and smoked until he reached the lone Customs official at the gate. Once there, he hoisted the valise he carried to the counter and opened it without being asked.

A sleepy-eyed man with a thick, drooping mustache and a tattered uniform barely glanced at the motley array of clothes the valise contained.

"Passaporte, por favor."

Carter handed him the Cavendish papers and lit yet another cigarette.

"Tem alcoólicas, senhor?"

"One bottle," Carter answered in Portuguese.

"Cigarettes?"

"Only two packs."

"The reason for your visit to Macao, Senhor, uh . . . Cavendish?"

"Gambling and a woman . . . if one can be found."

The smile was a leer. "In Macao, *senhor*, that will not be hard."

Carter thought he was home free, but at the last moment—probably because Cavendish was obviously a European—the officer decided to be polite and accommodating. He snapped the valise shut and hoisted it back toward Carter's waiting hands.

It never arrived.

It was written all over the man's face: a mere bundle of clothes would never heft with the weight of this valise.

The reason for the weight was the amount of steel secreted in the false bottom of the bag. Besides his 9mm Luger, Wilhelmina, and four extra clips, there was a British Mark V Sten submachine gun, a specially chambered barrel for 9mm parabellum slugs, four fully loaded thirty-two-round box magazines, five flash grenades, and a pound of plastique explosives.

"*Um momento, senhor.*"

The Customs official reset the valise on the counter, unsnapped it, and began digging in the clothes. Beneath them, he found ten quarts of expensive, duty-free scotch.

"One bottle, *senhor* . . . ?"

"A slip of memory," Carter replied, placing his hands by the other man's atop the valise and rolling the fingers open.

Tightly rolled and rubber-banded in each hand was a roll of Hong Kong dollars, all in tens.

The mustachioed man's hands moved like two darting mongeese. The bills had barely disappeared into his pockets before a stamp was slapped on the bag.

"Have a nice day in Macao, *senhor*."

Carter walked to the taxi stand whistling.

In the Estoril, he walked through the huge, ornate lobby until he found the public rest rooms.

In a locked stall, before a hand mirror propped on his knees, he removed Silas Cavendish. Ten minutes later he emerged, his shaven head sporting a fine fuzz of an emerging crew cut and a black, drooping mustache on his upper lip.

"Any room will do; I don't have a reservation. Only came down from Hong Kong for one night, test my luck at the casino, you know."

The desk clerk smiled, barely glanced at his passport, and produced a key. "Certainly, Mr. Cavendish. The hotel is crowded, but a room can always be found."

The Hong Kong fifty had disappeared from the passport when he handed it back.

Carter pressed another note into the bellman's hand and grabbed the valise himself. "I can handle it, thank you."

"Oh, Senhor Cavendish . . . !"

It was the desk clerk, waving a white envelope.

"Yes?"

"This was left for you early this morning."

"Thank you."

From the grin on the man's face, Carter guessed that a very large tip had accompanied the envelope.

This nearly bald man with the cold eyes and the ridiculous mustache was exactly the kind of guest hotel employees loved.

In his room, Carter threw the key and bag on the bed and ripped open the envelope. In it was a note, handwritten, and obviously by a woman.

My name is Ursula. We have a mutual friend, a captain. The captain has contacted me that his first plan for a meeting is impossible. However, I have the information you required.

Leave Macao on the Lisboa Highway. Go to its end and turn right. There is a small, unnamed road leading toward Penha Point. You will see it in the distance. Three kilometers short of the point, there is a narrow road to your left leading to the beach. My bungalow is right on the water, the last of five.

You may come any time this afternoon.

Carter reread the letter twice. It could be a trick, or a trap, or it could be for real.

He really didn't have much of a choice.

Back in the bedroom, he peeled out of his tie, shirt, and jacket. In their place, he donned a billowy sport shirt with a square cut that could be worn loose outside his pants.

From the false bottom of the valise, he took Wilhelmina. After checking her loads, he jammed the Luger into the waistband at the small of his back and headed for the door.

Two blocks from the Estoril, he stopped at a small shop and rented a motorbike. The papers and the deposit took nearly a half hour.

It was one o'clock, with the sun high over Macao and the Chinese mainland, when he hit the Lisboa Highway.

Whoever you are, Ursula, here I come!

The sea was calm. It stretched without swell or motion toward a band of stubborn fog lying on the far horizon. A few small boats were out; miniature whitecaps rolled in, breaking and crisping along the edge of the shore.

Carter slowed as he drove past the house, looking around carefully. An overhead garage door was lifted, and he could see a Mercedes convertible.

Whoever Ursula was, she had a bank account.

He rolled on for a couple of hundred yards to a place where he could turn around, then he rode back and parked across the way. Cutting the engine, he sat and looked for a long moment at the low house with its pebbled roof and the ivy-thick lawn that had been salvaged from the sand. The slow surge and boom of surf muttered behind the stillness.

He got off the motorbike and walked across the lawn to the house. Curtains were drawn across the windows. When he thumbed the button, he heard a door chime sound deep within the house, and though he rang a second time, the door remained closed. He turned and went along the flagged walk that rounded the house and led to the low-walled patio at the rear. As he approached the gate, strains of music reached him. And when he lifted the latch and pushed the gate open, he saw her.

She was stretched out on a lounge chair in the sun, her head in the shade of a beach umbrella. He saw a smooth, bare arm flung relaxed over the edge of the chaise and long legs stretched out before her, one slim, brown ankle crossed over the other. On the wrought-iron table beside her, next to a pile of magazines and papers, a transistor radio was pouring out a deep, rhythmic beat . . . explanation enough of why she hadn't heard the summons of the door chime. Nor did she turn at the sound of the gate's closing.

Carter walked forward, and as he rounded the umbrella, he saw that the music and the heavy heat had put her to sleep. She was sunbathing in nothing but a scarlet silk bikini—or, rather, in a part of one. Gasping, he halted in midstride. What might be called the top half—a mere scrap of bright material—had been discarded and lay beside the radio.

His breath clogged in his throat as he stood looking down at her, at the golden beauty of her. Apparently she had been tanning like this for some time, because there was no strap line to mar the tawny breasts. He could see the barest line of snow-white flesh where the bikini bottom touched her rounded belly low beneath the navel.

He took two more steps before he realized that the eyes weren't shut, only slitted. She wasn't asleep. Quite the opposite, she was very much awake and had been watching his every move.

He was five feet from the chaise when her hand slipped under the pillow beneath her head and came back out with a Webley .45 in it. The looked like a cannon in her small fist, but she held it unwaveringly, the muzzle pointed directly at his gut.

"That's far enough."

"Are you Ursula?"

"I could be. Who are you?"

"Cavendish . . . Silas Cavendish."

"If you're Cavendish, you have a letter."

"If you're Ursula, you wrote it. Who's our mutual friend?"

"A captain. Let me see the letter."

He handed it over. She took it very carefully by one corner, so Carter had no chance to grab her wrist and throw off her aim.

She was good, he thought as he watched her quickly peruse the letter with one eye while keeping the other on him.

Now he knew why it was handwritten. What better identification than a letter in one's own hand? Very tough to duplicate on short notice.

She nodded, smiled, and the Webley disappeared back under the pillow.

"Your woman described you differently to Lars . . . older, with gray hair and a mustache."

"Lars who?" Carter asked.

"Johannson."

Satisfied, Carter moved into a chair beside the chaise. "In the business I'm in, a change of appearance often comes with a change of underwear."

"And what business would that be?"

"You really don't need to know . . . do you?"

"No, not really."

"You have awesome breasts," Carter said casually, jolting her. She dropped her eyes, then reached for the wispy top on the concrete. "What happened that Captain Johannson couldn't meet me in the casino?" he asked while she was preoccupied.

She didn't bite, and quickly regained her cool and the leadership of the conversation. "Let's go inside."

The woman stood and moved past Carter with a ground-eating stride. He followed. They skirted the edge of the swimming pool, the reflection of her legs dancing in the blue water. Up a short flight of steps and beyond a blond wood door, they stepped into a living room done in relentless modern, all chrome and white.

"Make yourself comfortable. Drink?"

"Just a Perrier and lime, if you have it. It looks like it may be a long day and an even longer night."

She fixed his, then poured vodka over ice for herself. On her way back with the drinks, she grabbed a sketch pad from the bar.

"Usually, when the captain makes a run like this out of Hong Kong—particularly aboard the *Tokyo Star* and to Macao—it is an overnight trip. That is why he thought it would be no trouble to meet you in the hotel casino. He goes there often."

"But this time it's get the goods and go right back to Victoria."

"Yes."

She pulled an ottoman close to his chair and tore a few pages from the sketch pad before sipping her drink. Carter looked at the shadow of her lashes across her cheek, the smooth line of her arm raising the glass, the movement of her throat as she drank.

She didn't fit with what he knew of Johannson. He told her so and asked, "What's the connection?"

"He is my father . . . and my business partner. Just as I need to know nothing of your particular business, you need know nothing of ours. Suffice it to say that his master's ticket is very important to our profits."

Carter nodded, smiled, and said nothing. Their smuggling was the colonial authorities' problem. He had bigger fish to fry.

"I am assuming you have my father's papers of reinstatement from the Mariners Board or you wouldn't be here."

"That's a good assumption," Carter said. He lifted his pant leg, unwound the handkerchief holding an envelope to his ankle, and passed it to her.

Ursula Johannson perused them thoroughly but quickly. It was obvious that she knew exactly what to look for.

"Excellent. We will keep our part of the bargain." She set the envelope aside and began arranging the sheets from the sketch pad. "This is a sketch of the inner harbor. Here is the pier where the *Tokyo Star* will dock."

"Does the captain have an ETA?"

"Yes, around ten o'clock tonight. They will probably be there no longer than an hour. When the crates were brought up from Hong Kong the last time, my father said that there were two of them. He has no reason to believe that the number will change."

"How do I know they will be there?"

"I'm coming to that. There is a bar, here, on the top floor of this building about three blocks from the pier. Do you have field glasses?"

"I didn't bring them."

"Buy a pair this afternoon. From eight on, stay in your hotel room. I can see the point of the bay from my porch, out there. When I see the *Tokyo Star* round the point and head in, I will call you at the hotel."

"And I head for the bar."

"Exactly. It's called the Mariner. Bribe someone for a table by the window. When you see that the goods are loaded, come back here at once."

"Here?"

"Yes." She selected another sketch. "Here is a layout of the bay all the way around to Penha Point. Right here, just beyond the point, a marina is being constructed. It is far from finished, but there are several piers in place. It is the last chance between Macao and Hong Kong for a junk to put into for repairs without squabbling in the open sea with Chinese gunboats."

"Something is going to happen to the *Tokyo Star*?"

"My father has already weakened the rudder stays. They

will be strained again coming into the bay. My father is a good seaman. The rudder will become all but useless just beyond Penha Point.''

Carter went over the sketch several times. "Can I get to the marina overland, from here . . . or here?''

"Yes, perhaps in the daytime, but at night it would be very risky. Chinese patrols pay little attention to the boundaries after dark. They often cross them at night, looking for smugglers. If you were Chinese, they would merely ask for a token bribe and let you go on your way. But . . .''

"I understand. That's why you want me to come back here.''

"Exactly,'' the woman replied. "I have a small fishing boat, twelve feet, one mast. Can you sail?''

Carter nodded.

"Good, but it has a two-and-a-half horsepower outboard anyway. The boat will get you to the marina. What you do, and how you do it, is up to you. My father has requested only one thing.''

"And that is . . . ?''

"There are four in his crew besides your woman. These four men will be in the water working on the rudder. When your disturbance starts, they will swim to here, where I will pick them up.''

"And your father?''

"He will have a gun, loaded with blanks, and help Kim See Long and Luchan protect the goods. He is assuming, of course, that you will not kill him.''

"I shall be very selective. Kim See Long is the local hired gun?''

"Yes. He will have four of his men aboard the *Tokyo Star* as guards. Don't underestimate him or his men. They are good, all defectors from the Chinese army. Luchan uses them often.''

"Have you ever met Luchan?''

"I've seen him once.''

"Describe him to me."

Ursula gave a perfect description of Ishi Komuku. So now Carter knew the little assassin's Chinese identity.

Well, he thought, hopefully after tonight he would have no further use for it.

"I couldn't have come up with a better plan to get in myself," Carter commented. "As for getting the goods after I get in, that's up to me. Any suggestions on how I get out?"

"That depends."

She sat back, leaning on one elbow and studying Carter over the rim of her glass as she sipped the drink.

"On what?"

"You may load the goods in the boat and come back here. If there are none of Kim See Long's men left to follow you, I will let you dock. If they are around, anywhere, I will shoot you before you can tie up."

Carter smiled and nodded his agreement. "Fair enough. And I presume, for a certain fee, you would know how to get the woman, and myself, and the goods safely back to Hong Kong."

It was her turn to smile. "I would assume your presumption is about one hundred percent correct."

"One question."

"Yes?"

"Does Luchan—or any of his people—know about you, your relationship to the captain, or even of your existence?"

"No, not at all," she said firmly. "I am his safety valve."

"Good. In fact, excellent. May I take these?" He picked up the sketches.

"Of course."

"You can start making arrangements for the trip back to Hong Kong."

Ursula stood and moved with him toward the door. "You have a very high opinion of yourself."

"Very high," he replied. "I'll see you tonight, twice."

Across the road, he kicked the motorbike to life and rode

back into downtown Macao.

After depositing the little machine with one of the hotel attendants, he hit the street again and walked until he found the old quarter.

In different stores, he bought a baggy black shirt, a pair of black, baggy, pajama-type bottoms, and dark canvas shoes. The last stop was for a conical straw hat resembling those worn by every junksman and fisherman in the bay, and a compact, watertight bag.

On his return to the hotel, he made a detour down by the docks. He only had to consult Ursula's sketch once to locate the pier where the *Tokyo Star* would tie up that night.

Across the warehouse building behind the pier was a large sign in Portuguese, English, and Chinese: CHANSUNG IMPORT-EXPORT LTD. OF MACAO.

Chansung owned the *Tokyo Star,* and they, in turn, were owned by Kulo Electronics of Japan.

As he walked back to the Estoril, Carter mulled this over in his mind. He was pretty sure now that when he finally hit Japan and came down on Charlie Loo, he would locate the man through Kulo.

TEN

It was 9:10 sharp, thirty minutes after Ursula Johannson's call, when the Killmaster walked into the Mariner bar.

He had prepaid the hotel, so there was no need to check out. The valise and random clothes had gone down the disposal chute. All but four of the bottles of scotch had been left in the room.

Two of those four bottles were now in the hands of a wise-eyed little urchin down in the street, guarding the motorbike with his life. They were half the boy's payment. The other half was in the watertight bag Carter carried, along with the hardware from the false bottom of the valise.

"The bar, *senhor*, or a table?"

"A table, *por favor*."

"Of course." The Maître d' headed toward the bowels of the room.

"Ah, a table by the window, if you don't mind."

"I am sorry, *senhor*, but at this time of the evening . . ."

"I love to watch the bay," Carter said, pressing a large bill into the man's hand.

"I understand. Follow me, please."

119

At one glance, Carter could tell that the Mariner was overrated and overpriced. There had been an attempt to create a South Seas atmosphere, with a ship's mahogany bar and varnished bamboo mats on the walls.

None of it worked, but the table had a commanding view of part of the bay and the entire waterfront area.

He ordered a bottle of the most expensive wine on the menu, along with one glass. That would keep them off his back about dinner. When it came, he unlimbered the binoculars he had purchased from a huckster outside the hotel entrance. For only a few more Hong Kong dollars, he could have gotten a camera to go along with them.

They weren't the best, but they were strong enough for his purposes.

He sipped the first glass until it was empty, refilled, and lit a cigarette.

It was just after ten when the *Tokyo Star* came into sight. They were about two hundred yards out from the pier, but already the sails were falling, and Carter could tell that the junk's diesel had been fired up.

Johannson was good. He headed right for the pier and, at the last second, skittered the big junk sideways. It settled against the pier's rubber bumpers with a kiss, and three crew members leaped over the side to tie her up.

Carter scanned them and the others scurrying across the deck. He found Luchan, alias Komuku, Johannson, and another man barking orders that looked to be the hotshot Kim See Long.

He couldn't locate Soo Lee, but then he knew that she would probably have been given myriad chores to do below decks.

There was no mixing up the crew with the hoody types. The latter, other than their leader, all wore black pants, tight, and dark, bulky jackets. The jackets were much too heavy for the weather but perfect for concealing the iron beneath them.

As soon as the junk tied up and the gangway was let down,

two of the black jackets hit the pier. They herded the crew
back aboard and took up positions on each side of the gangway.

Komuku was next. When he hit the pier, he paused and
turned. Johannson and the leather jackets' headman—
dressed in a summer-weight suit with a red shirt and black
tie—were at the rail.

They exchanged words, and Komuku took off. Carter was
able to follow him up the steps to the port street and into a
cab.

Dammit, he thought, *I might have nailed the goods at the
main source. But no, that's when, during the transfer, they
would be most alert.*

This was the best way. That is, if Ursula and Johannson
were on the up and up.

Back at the junk. Quiet. Smoking. Watching.

He set the binoculars on the table and rubbed his eyes.

"More wine, *senhor*?"

"What? . . . Oh, no, this is fine."

A half pack of cigarettes later, with only about three
fingers left in the bottom of the wine bottle, the lights of a
black Jaguar sedan came out of an alley and turned toward the
Chansung pier.

It was 11:30.

It was quick—no conversation, no wasted motion.

The driver stayed in the Jag. Komuku got out and opened
the trunk. The two guards came forward. One to a crate, they
headed back to the junk.

They were barely aboard, with Komuku right behind
them, when the crew was hauling up the gangway and casting
off.

Carter quickly paid his bill and headed for the street.

Clouds scudded across the moon in a crazy jigsaw pattern,
giving the road a patchy, light-dark, light-dark effect.

Carter made good time to the narrow road that turned down

to the beach and Ursula Johannson's bungalow. At the turn
he killed the bike's headlight, and halfway down the hill he
flipped the ignition switch, silencing the little engine.

He had barely glided to a halt in the carport beside the
Mercedes, when she materialized in the doorway leading to
the patio.

"You made good time."

"No traffic once I hit the main road," he replied, grabbing
the bag and moving toward her.

"They are about in the middle of the bay, and already the
steering looks a little erratic."

"How do you know that?"

"I can see it," she replied, a bit of disdain in her voice.
"The long-range scope in my bedroom window is fixed with
alternate lenses, night viewers. Follow me."

More and more, Carter thought, little Ursula and her daddy
amazed him. They were far from amateurs in this business.

He followed her on a narrow, winding path down to the
beach. She wore a skintight black wet suit that hugged every
curve and hollow of her long, lithe body. Now and then,
when the moon would cruise behind a cloud, Carter almost
lost her against the foliage.

At last his shoes found sand. He turned back and looked for
the house. Darkness. The beach lay like an empty gray carpet
before them.

"This way!"

The little wooden shed was only thirty yards away, but
Carter hadn't seen it. Ursula unlocked the door, and they both
slid inside.

"Is there a light?"

"Yes."

It came on instantly, a small-watt bulb painted red, probably with nail polish.

Ursula didn't miss a trick.

There were two boats, one on each side of the narrow pier.
The fishing boat Carter was to use was low in the water, and

wide. The other was a sixteen-foot power launch, low and sleek. Carter guessed there was a very powerful Chrysler marine under the inboard canopy.

Without a word, they both went to work. Ursula jumped into the launch like a cat, and Carter attacked the contents of the bag.

Very carefully he undressed, leaving on only his shorts. He pulled on the black pajamas and laced the ties around his waist, up around his chest, and then tied them around his neck. To the ties he clipped the grenades and the plastique. He donned the blouse and filled its big pockets with the extra magazine for the Sten and Wilhelmina's clips.

"Be careful you don't fall overboard," Ursula said with a chuckle. "You'll sink like a rock."

He glanced up. She was just finishing the attachment of a B.S.A. 7.62mm heavy machine gun to a tripod on the bow of the launch. A small door opened in the highly polished wood, and out of it came a belt feed. As she was stringing the belt, she glanced up and saw Carter watching her.

"Pretty potent."

"I take no chances . . . not any more."

She flipped the cover catch down over the breech and rigged the gun for firing. She was strapping the Webley he had seen earlier that day around her waist when Carter went back to his own chores.

He checked the spring release on Hugo—the razor-sharp stiletto he wore attached to his right forearm in a chamois sheath—and then attached a clip holster to the pajama's waistband at the small of his back. When Wilhelmina's silencer was in place, he checked the load and slid the Luger into the holster.

It took him less than thirty seconds to strip the stock from the Sten and attach one of the thirty-two-round magazines. He then slid the gun up under his blouse and used the stock clips to secure it to the ties around his chest.

He tested the swing of the weapon under the blouse by

walking up and down the pier several times. When he was satisfied that it couldn't be detected that way, and that the barrel was completely hidden by the bottom of the blouse, he unhooked it and set it carefully in the bottom of the boat.

"Ready," he said.

"Good. You go first. Use the engine as far as the point. From there in, you'd better rig the sails. No fisherman worth his salt around here would waste gas when there is a steady wind, like there is tonight."

Carter only nodded. He slipped the bowline and stepped aboard. Slowly he hand-walked the boat out from under cover.

"One more thing . . ."

"Yes?"

"You have a plan to keep up my father's pretense?"

"Yes," Carter said. "One magazine for the Luger is filled with blank cartridges. He'll know what to do when the time comes."

"Thank you," she whispered.

"Thank you," Carter replied and pulled the start cord on the engine.

It roared to life, and in no time he was moving at a steady five knots along the coast.

Because of the hour, there were more boats coming out than going in, but Carter was able to mingle and slide into a pier five places away from the moored *Tokyo Star*.

She had been easy to spot from the time he rounded the point and hoisted sail. Auxilliary lights on the stern of the junk itself, and on the pier, beamed down into the water around the big rudder.

The closer he got, the easier it was to discern the bobbing heads in the water doing the repairs. One black-pajamaed figure was topside in the stern, lowering and raising materials and tools in a bucket to the crewmen below.

Carter guessed that would be Soo Lee. He could also hear

the steady throb of a gas-powered portable generator, and he
hoped that its master switch was close enough to her hand to
kill it when the time came.

He slid into the midst of a queue of boats of similar size and
tied up to a stringer line.

Three boats down, an old fisherman sat cross-legged in
front of a pot fire in the middle of his boat. Carter could smell
the old man's food cooking and barely nodded when a hand
was raised in greeting.

The offer had been made to share but had been rejected.
Without even a shrug, the old man went back to watching his
fire.

Carter checked and then rechecked his arms. When he was
completely satisfied that he could get to everything in a split
second, he hoisted a roll of netting to his left shoulder and set
off.

He shuffled his pace in the slow, rolling gait of a man who
spends long hours balanced upright in a moving boat. The
nearer he got to the *Tokyo Star*, the more he weaved, seach-
ing out shadows.

He was moving in facing the bow, with the bright lights at
the stern on the other side of the two sentries by the gangway.

Without altering his pace, the Killmaster slipped his right
hand up and under the baggy blouse. His fingers closed over
the butt of Wilhelmina, and then she was out, moving up into
the obscurity of the netting on his shoulder.

The moon chose that moment—when he was about forty
yards from the junk's bow—to come out full. Neither of the
guards were paying him any attention, but still he slowed his
pace slightly.

The closer he got, the more his eyes flicked upward,
scanning the rail and the two decks of the junk.

His luck was holding. Now if it would just hold for another
full minute. . . .

Light flowed from behind curtains in the aft cabin. There
was a single dim lantern hanging in the bowlines, illuminat-

ing a third sentry with his attention riveted out to sea. Other than his silhouette against the moon, there was not another soul to be seen on deck.

Both of the pier sentries were smoking. They were about five yards apart, and both of them were watching the men in the water.

Carter was ten steps away now, his finger curling around the trigger of the silenced Luger, taking up the slack, getting ready to fire.

One of the men turned. His face was bland, but as the Killmaster drew nearer, his features took on a look of suspicion.

He held up his hands as if to halt Carter, and when the Killmaster kept coming, the suspicion in the face changed to open hostility and his right hand disappeared beneath the dark jacket he wore.

His hand, full of U.S. Army issue Colt .45, was just coming into the light when Carter fired. Two 9mm slugs made a mess of the man's face. He had barely hit the wood of the pier when his buddy caught onto the *pffftt* sounds that had sent his partner there.

He, too, went for a piece from under his jacket, but by then the net had rocketed over his head. He made one sound, a garbled grunt, as Wilhelmina came down across his temple.

He rocked, still on his feet, and staggered forward. Carter twisted the net in his left hand, using the man's own momentum to swing him around. At the same time, he raised the muzzle of the silencer until it was cushioned against the upturned collar of the jacket.

This one only took one slug, up from the top of the spine and right into the center of his brain.

He pitched forward, and Carter eased the body into the water with the net. When he released it, a face appeared not six inches from the corpse.

"Go!" Carter breathed.

The narrow almond eyes got suddenly round. The head

nodded, and he was off. Within seconds, Carter could see wriggling bodies swimming like hell for the darkness beyond the lights.

He looked up, over the bow rail. Soo Lee had discarded her straw hat. Her face gleamed in the light.

They made ten seconds of sign language, and then Carter rolled the first sentry to the edge of the pier with his foot.

Again he looked up.

Soo Lee nodded.

Carter kicked.

The lights went out the instant the body splashed into the water.

Carter hit the gangway at a dead run. The bow sentry had already come over from the starboard side. He was moving aft at a good pace, with an old Enfield across his chest and a puzzled look on his face.

Carter hit the top of the gangway three seconds, six paces, after the man passed. Purposely, he banged Wilhelmina's butt against the rail.

The man whirled, cursing and bringing the muzzle of the Enfield down.

One hundred and eight grains of flat-nosed lead hit him just above his right eyebrow. The bullet flattened as it struck the hard bone of the skull, mushrooming out to more than double its original size. The bone fractured and gave way, fragments crashing off through the brain in all directions, mangling it beyond recognition, while the bullet itself angled off, broke the skull at the rear, and finally exited.

The man was dead from the microsecond the lead slammed into his head, but he continued a half step forward before he toppled forward and hit the deck.

The Killmaster jumped forward and to the side to avoid the falling corpse. At the same time, he counted in his mind and crouched to check the lower deck crew quarters through an open porthole.

"Shit," he hissed.

There was a miscount. Right now there was a body count of three. That should have left one more besides Komuku and the gangster type, Kim See Long.

But there in the crew's quarters were three dark jackets playing Chinese dice.

A quick look aft told Carter that Soo Lee was in place.

He holstered Wilhelmina and unclipped the grenades. Bunching them with his right forearm against his chest, he pulled the pins and tossed them in, a millisecond apart.

By the time the first one went off, he had freed the Sten and was in place for their exit.

They came out screaming and empty-handed, all of them on fire.

Carter, with one knee on the deck, stitched them in turn and then whirled, covering the door of the aft cabin.

He saw the latch drop, and then the door parted just a crack. He brought the Sten up, pointing it at just the spot where a head would appear.

The door opened a little farther, a hand came out full of Webley, and then an arm.

The arm was encased in a dark material with a cuff of bright red.

Kim See Long.

"I'm here," Carter hissed.

The door slammed open, and the Webley spit orange. Three slugs whirred harmlessly above Carter's head.

The Killmaster squeezed off one burst that spread blue suit, red shirt, blood, and bone all over the exterior bulkhead. The man was sliding down in his own gore as Carter stitched him again across the chest for good measure.

Overkill?

Yeah, Carter thought, probably. But it was better than underkill.

He moved to the hatch and peered through the crack.

Komuku was behind a wooden desk, a .357 Ruger in one hand and a heavy Colt in the other. He was balanced on his elbows and knees, with the guns raking the open hatch.

"It's me, Komuku. Carter."

The little Japanese cut loose with both guns at the sound of Carter's voice. Wood splinters flew everywhere as a half-dozen slugs ripped into and through the hatch.

Carter had already moved back a half-dozen paces.

"Soo Lee!"

The lady's name had barely left Carter's lips when the glass of the cabin's aft window shattered. Slugs from her Sten ripped across the deck, inches from where Komuku crouched.

He was leveling off, turning, trying to find a target beyond the wrecked glass, when Carter hit the door firing. Soo Lee opened up again at the same time.

The crossfire was withering, and Komuku knew it. He dropped the guns and flattened out.

Carter did a quick recon. The door to the head was closed, but there was light beneath it.

"Who's in there?" he barked.

Komuku didn't even look up. Carter turned and sprayed the door near the very top.

"I'm coming out . . . I'm coming out!"

The door opened, and Captain Lars Johannson emerged with his hands on his head.

"Stay like that!" Carter snapped and turned back to Komuku. "Get up!"

He did, smiling. "I assume the reports of your death with the policeman and the woman were exaggerated."

He was very cool, and very calm, and very oily. It was all Carter could do not to squeeze the Sten and see what the man would look like plastered across the bulkhead.

Instead, the Killmaster matched his smile. "It's been an interesting game. I've studied you all the way from the States."

The assassin's eyebrows went up on that one. "You were on the same plane . . . ?"

Carter then gave him a rundown on every move Komuku had made since landing in Kowloon.

"I see. Then I see my usefulness here is over."

"Everybody's is," Carter replied. He rattled off the info they had on the medical clinic, Connie Chu, and, lastly, the files. "So you see, Komuku, we've got it all . . . all, that is, except Charlie Loo."

Komuku's grin widened. "Charlie Loo? I have never heard the name."

"Haven't you, now?" Carter said. "We'll see about that when I get you in a quiet place, all alone, just the two of us."

"Do you have them?"

It was Soo Lee's voice from somewhere in the darkness outside the cabin.

"Yeah," Carter yelled. "Come on down to the main deck and cover them coming out!"

"Right."

He heard the padding sound of her feet and floated his eyes around the cabin.

"Where are the crates?"

"What crates?" Komuku replied, his dead eyes saying nothing and never moving from Carter's hands on the Sten.

"Please try it," the Killmaster hissed. "The crates I saw you load in Macao."

When the Japanese said nothing, Carter turned to Johannson.

"Who are you?"

"Johannson. I am captain and pilot."

"Where are the crates you brought aboard in Macao?"

Johannson didn't blink. He also didn't speak. Carter sprayed a neat swath of splinters six inches above his head.

Johannson still didn't blink, nor did he speak.

Enough of this, Carter thought, and backed away.

"Outside, both of you!" he barked. "Soo Lee?"

"Yes."

"They're coming out."

"Right!"

"Komuku, you first."

The smaller man moved, and Johannson fell in behind him. Just before he reached the hatch, the captain inclined his head and blinked his eyes toward the bunks on the far side of the cabin.

Carter blinked in return.

"Soo Lee, you have them."

"I can take them both with one burst," came the confident reply.

Carter strode to the two tiered bunks and gingerly moved them. Carefully, he ran his hand over the planks of the deck. A small section—one plank about eight inches long—gave a little under his probing fingers.

Using Wilhelmina, he pried it up, and smiled.

Under it was the iron ring of a trapdoor. And under the trapdoor he found the two crates. One by one, he pulled them out. In their place he put two charges of the plastique from under his blouse, their timer-detonators set for twenty minutes.

"How are you doing?" Soo Lee called.

"Got 'em!"

Carter slung the Sten over his shoulder and tugged the crates toward the hatch. Neither of them was overly heavy, but then, he reasoned, the originals of pieces of blackmail material and probably a microfilm of something on five or six men wouldn't weigh very much.

He dropped one by Johannson and one by Komuku, and pulled the Luger from under his blouse. At this range, the handgun was preferable.

"Grab 'em!"

Johannson picked up one of the crates. Komuku didn't move, the inscrutable smile plastered across his face.

The Killmaster sighted Wilhelmina in both hands and repeated the command. When the assassin still didn't move, Carter squeezed one off.

Komuku screamed as the bullet passed through the palm of his left hand. He then fell to his knees, cursing and holding the injured hand out in front of him as if he could command away the tremendous pain.

Carter moved forward and yanked the man to his feet by the back of his jacket at the neck. At the same time, he laid the muzzle of the Luger along Komuku's crotch.

"Next one'll blow away your balls."

"My hand . . ."

"You've still got a good one. Pick it up with that."

Sweat streamed into the little Japanese's hate-filled eyes as he bent toward the crate. He struggled it to his shoulder with his good hand, and all of them moved to the gangway, with Komuku leaving a steady trail of blood from his wound.

Soo Lee went first, with Carter in the rear and the two crate bearers in the middle. As they moved down the gangway, Carter ejected Wilhelmina's clip and inserted the one he had loaded with blanks.

Johannson had barely set down his crate on the very edge of the pier, when he made his move.

The burly captain lifted a trouser leg on his way up and whirled on Carter with an automatic in his hand. He got off one shot while the Killmaster fired three.

Johannson was a good actor. He emoted a gurgling scream and toppled from the pier into the water. Carter ran forward and, for effect, dropped another slug into the supposedly struggling body.

Johannson made an "O" of two fingers, and was already diving underwater and swimming away.

"Nick . . ."

Carter whirled, bringing up the Luger, then realized it was useless. Komuku was as fast as a striking cobra. By the time Carter had unlimbered the Sten, the other man was over Soo Lee like a blanket, using her body to shield his.

He had his arms over her shoulders and was struggling to relieve her of the Mark II she had.

For a split second, she got the sub out of his grasp and made the only decision a seasoned agent could make.

She heaved the gun toward Carter.

Mentally, Komuku was just as fast.

His arms came up to fold expertly around Soo Lee's neck. She cried out in pain as the pressure on her throat was applied.

"You know the hold, Carter?"

"I know it."

"Then you know it's a stalemate, bastard."

He was already back-pedaling toward the long pier of small fishing boats. As he moved, he continued to keep the woman's body in front of his own.

It was impossible for the Killmaster to get off a clean shot.

He took two steps forward. All that accomplished was another bone-jarring scream of pain from Soo Lee.

Komuku was incredibly strong for his size and equally agile. Somehow he managed to unhook one of the boats and manipulate himself and Soo Lee into the stern without risking any spot of his body that would give Carter a kill shot.

With the hold Komuku had, Carter knew it would have to be a kill shot. Anything else, and Komuku would snap her neck like a twig.

He felt like an ass, totally worthless with the powerful Sten in his hands, as Komuku backed the boat out and around the *Tokyo Star*.

Komuku had just passed out of sight around the junk, when the plastique Carter had set exploded. Boards, hardware, and saffron flame lurched into the night sky.

Carter had been snookered and he knew it. There was nothing he could do. If he tried to follow, Komuku would kill Soo Lee the second he got too close.

There was an alternative . . . a bargain, a trade.

But that would have to come later.

Right now, the explosion and inferno of the *Tokyo Star* would have everybody within a mile down to the marina.

Carter moved. He hoisted the crates and made for his own boat at a dead run.

He was just shoving off, when he looked up and saw the old man a few boats down, slowly forking food from a rice bowl into his mouth with chopsticks.

Obviously the old man had seen everything that had occurred on the pier, and at that moment, he was bathed in the light from the flames devouring the *Tokyo Star*.

He didn't even look up from his dinner at Carter.

ELEVEN

With the help of Ursula Johannson and her father, Carter was back in Hong Kong by five in the morning.

Ursula had picked up the crew of the *Tokyo Star* and Lars Johannson. While swimming away, the captain had suspected that something had misfired.

An hour later, Carter had arrived at the bungalow and told them what had transpired. He also told them that he wanted to maintain hourly contact with them. Why? Because he would most probably need further help from them.

Ursula protested. "We have completed our part of the bargain. We can do no more."

Carter explained matter-of-factly that as long as Charlie Loo was alive, Captain Johannson didn't have a prayer of staying alive.

It was Carter's ace-in-the-hole. After a hurried, very private consultation on the patio, father and daughter agreed to cooperate . . . for a fee.

Carter didn't mind. Mercenaries often make the best soldiers.

He had barely hit the hotel in Hong Kong before he was on

the phone to Commander Jarvis, again rousing him from a sound sleep.

The Englishman practically went into apoplexy when Carter told him the tale of the night's happenings.

"All well and good, Commander, but we have the source of Charlie Loo's power . . . the files."

"And the woman?"

"I have a hunch that Komuku won't touch her, at least not yet. She's a bargaining chip."

Jarvis sighed, resigned now to the Wild West approach Carter took to settle affairs. "What next, then?"

"I want every piece of paper, every piece of microfilm, every shred in those crates copied. Can you get to Macao quick? . . . a helicopter?"

"Of course."

"Good."

Carter told him where to pick up the crates and what else to do with them.

"Also, I want it leaked to every underworld type in Hong Kong that Nick Carter is here, that I'll be checking into the Regent sometime in the morning, and I'm ready to deal. The captain and his daughter will do the same in Macao."

"You're changing hotels?"

"Of course. They'll spot me and cover me from then on."

"Who is 'they'?"

"I would imagine Connie Chu, for one. Right now, with Komuku gone to ground, she's the link to Charlie Loo. If I know Charlie, nobody down here will make a move without his okay."

Carter hung up, then dialed the lovers' aerie that Mrs. Bruno Falkner shared with Lin Duong.

"Yes?"

"Lin, this is Carter. Anything from Patrice on the clinic?"

"Nothing. She has gone over the bank withdrawals, the deposits, and the long-distance telephone receipts. There is no connection at all between her husband and Japan."

"So it looks as though Komuku is the only link between the doctor and Connie Chu."

"It would seem so."

"Sit tight. Call me here if you get anything. Later this morning I'll be moving to the Regent under my own name."

"You think that's wise?"

"Now I do. Later."

The connection had hardly been broken before Carter was back on the horn to Jarvis's office and a very weary Giles Gordon.

"My God, my God, my God," was Gordon's only comment as Carter brought him up-to-date.

"The Commander will be calling you in a few minutes, I'm sure, to bring you the very latest info on all this. Meanwhile, what have you got?"

"We put a tail on Ashami Okamoto the minute he got off the plane from Tokyo. He checked into a hotel, did some shopping—all the normal things—and then, just before office hours ended, he hit the clinic."

"And . . . ?"

"And he delivered the latest shipment. The woman with Komuku arrived just after he left. We tailed her as far as Connie Chu's gate, and then, just like you said, we picked her up. She had four rolls of microfilm . . . very interesting stuff."

"Interrogation?"

"Nothing. She's like a clam and hard as nails."

Carter checked his watch. It was almost seven in the morning.

"Pick him up when he comes down for breakfast. If he orders from room service, go up with the tray and take him then."

"Righto. On what charge?"

"Protective custody. If he screams too loud, play him the Komuku-Charlie Loo tape. That should convince him."

"And you?"

"A couple of hours' sleep. My mind's a vegetable. But call me if anything pops."

"Will do."

Carter hung up, checked the chain on the door, and fell across the bed. Fumbling with one hand, he set the travel alarm and went out like a light.

It was 10:10 when Carter was blasted awake. He was consumed with one overwhelming desire: to throw the obnoxious little clock into Hong Kong Bay.

He ordered breakfast from room service, and a half hour later was showered, dressed, fed, and on his way to the Regent.

The Regent Hotel was first class, opulent, and expensive. The lobby near the doors was crowded, near the desk sparse: a few check-outs, a somber woman behind the desk registering early arrivals, and an obese lounger with a dark mustache who was entirely too absorbed in his newspaper.

"Carter . . . Nicholas Carter," he said a little too loudly to the desk clerk. "I phoned for reservations this morning from the Shangri-La."

"Yes, sir. The length of your stay?"

"Open, as long as my business takes."

The paper ruffled in the mustachioed man's hands.

"Yes, sir. All we have is a suite."

"That's fine."

"Your passport, please?"

Carter went through the formalities of checking in, then followed a young boy to the huge bank of elevators. Just before stepping into the car, he glanced back at the solo chair by the desk.

It was vacant.

The fat man had crossed to the desk and was poring over the registration card Carter had signed. He nodded to the clerk, smiled, and waddled his bulk toward a row of telephones.

I do believe, Carter thought, *that I will soon be announced to Madame Connie Chu*.

The phone rang just as the door closed behind the bellboy.

"Carter here."

"Gordon. We picked up Ashami Okamoto. He's a very nervous gentleman."

"You played the tape?"

"We did. He's talking as fast as our tape recorder is running."

"Let me guess. Kulo Electronics is a front set up by Charlie Loo to broker and collect info from the men in the other firms he's blackmailing."

"You've got it. Okamoto claims he's an innocent victim of the blackmail himself, but he also admits to becoming a millionaire in the last two years."

"Keep him talking, and keep him on ice. What about the girl you picked up outside Connie Chu's?"

"She's a hard one. We threw everything at her and she wouldn't budge."

Carter's mind clicked. "How close is she to Komuku?"

"Not that close, if you're thinking of trading her for Soo Lee. Definitely not Komuku's type: short, fat, ugly, but loyal . . . for money. She's also smart. Says she didn't know what she was delivering. She'll probably get off if we can't get anything else to hold her on. The locals are already grumbling about our interference with the Victoria constabulary."

"Hang on to her as long as you can. Anything from the streets?"

"We've put the word out that you want to talk. Nothing back yet."

Carter smiled. "I'll probably hear before you do."

"The Commander is in."

"Yeah?"

"Hot, very hot. Thinks you should have let us in on the *Tokyo Star* business."

"What do you think?"

Gordon chuckled. "I'm rather a lone wolf at times myself, old boy. There's only so much a bureaucracy can do, then a lad sometimes must take matters into his own hands."

"Good man," Carter sighed. "Keep him calm if you can. I'll call you."

"Righto."

Carter ordered an enormous lunch and stuffed himself. He knew he would need all the energy he could get for the twenty-four hours to come.

One way or another, he was going to find out where Komuku was holding Soo Lee. The last resort would be Connie Chu herself, but hopefully something else would pay off first.

The phone rang again as he was pouring his third cup of coffee.

"Yes?"

"Nick, I'm so happy to hear that your demise was a figment of someone's imagination!"

Connie Chu.

He would know that low, sultry, barely accented voice anywhere, from the bottom of a well, or beside him in bed.

"Hello, Connie. I hear the years have treated you well."

"Financially, yes. The rest? . . . A few lines here and there, a sag or two. Really, I can't complain."

"I'm surprised you went back into business with Charlie," Carter growled. "I mean, considering that it was you who helped bust him up in Vietnam."

"Is this phone tapped?"

"No."

"I believe you . . . your word has always been good. That's why Charlie still trusts me. You never let anyone know that it was me who gave the information you needed."

"To save your own skin."

"A girl has to survive. It's a tough world, Nick."

Carter took a deep breath. It was a gamble. "Want to do it again, Connie?"

She laughed. It was a low, husky chuckle, really, and it said worlds to the Killmaster. Her words reinforced it.

"I'm afraid not this time. Charlie still holds all the cards."

"And you, Connie, always go with the winning hand."

"Of course, you know that. We have the woman, you have the files. *Touché.*"

"If I copy the files, I get to the men who are being blackmailed. That makes the files worthless to you."

"Very true. That is why we must inspect the crates before the transfer is made."

Carter's mind whirled. "They're specially sealed?"

"Yes . . . laser sealed. If the contact is broken, the whole mess goes sky-high. I assume, since you are alive to talk, you haven't broken the seals as yet. Don't! If you do, you lose both ways."

"I'll have to confer, you know that."

"I expected it. Suppose you ring me at five?"

"Five it is."

"Good. It's wonderful hearing your voice again, Nick. I haven't forgotten the good moments, believe me."

The phone went dead. Carter quickly broke his end of the connection and, like a wild man, dialed Jarvis's office.

A secretary answered.

"Giles Gordon . . . fast!"

"Yes, sir."

Carter inhaled a whole cigarette in three rasping gasps, the seconds screaming, as he waited.

"Gordon here."

"Gordon, Carter! Have you done anything with the crates yet?"

"Started, but they are oddly sealed. We've brought in an expert."

"Stop, right now!"

"What?"

"Get to him fast and stop him!"

The receiver dropped noisily to a desk top. Gordon was a good man. Someone like Nick Carter didn't scream for nothing, and he knew it.

"Done. What's up?" he said, coming back on the line.

"The crates have been laser sealed and booby-trapped. Charlie Loo doesn't take any chances. Don't touch them until you hear from me again!"

"They are refrigerated, in fact, on ice," Gordon replied, a slight quiver in his voice. "Also, we had a report from our man at the clinic. Nobody showed for work today."

"Damn," Carter muttered, wishing now that he would have agreed to a tail on Bruno Falkner. "Have you checked his house?"

"No, stayed away. Those were your instructions."

"Yeah, I know. Put someone on him now . . . if he hasn't already flown."

"Will do."

For the next two hours, Carter paced and smoked. If no word came in from the street or from any other source, he would have to deal with Connie Chu.

He knew how he would handle it . . . a bluff that really wasn't a bluff:

"I want the girl and I want the files, Connie. But the files are more important. Soo Lee is an agent. She gets paid to risk her skin."

"You're saying, Nick, that you would let the girl die?"

"That's what I'm saying. Of course, in exchange, I'll kill you . . . but that's the way it goes."

He was hoping it wouldn't come to that, because if the bottom line were reached, Carter knew that Soo Lee would be sacrificed.

That was the way of it, the way the game was played.

At 4:10, the phone rang and Carter pounced on it.

It was Lin Duong and she was hysterical, borderline crazy.

"Calm down, Lin, calm down. Patrice called?"

"Yes, and something is very wrong, I could tell!"

"Wrong? Okay, what did she say?"

"She gave me a grocery list!"

"What?"

"A grocery list . . ."

Here the girl broke down again. Carter tried to make out the words between the sobs but found it impossible.

"Shh, shh. Look, Lin, don't move. Stay right where you are."

"Oh, so afraid, am so afraid!"

"Yes, yes, I know, Lin. I'll be right there. For God's sake, don't do anything, and stay by the phone!"

In minutes, Carter was in a taxi lurching toward the peak tram. The tram would be far faster than trying to drive halfway up the summit through traffic.

He only hoped that when he got there he could make some sense out of what Patrice Falkner had told Lin Duong.

He exited the tram near Albert Road and walked around the peak to the enclave of houses that contained Patrice Falkner's bungalow.

Lin met him at the door. She was less hysterical, but her eyes were wide with fear.

It took nearly five minutes and several gulps from a brandy snifter before Carter had the girl calm enough to speak intelligibly about the call from Pat.

"I barely said hello, and she says, 'Wang Chow Market?' I laughed. I didn't know if it was a joke or what . . ."

Little bells were already ringing in Carter's brain. "Go on. What did she say then? And try to remember everything, every word."

"I don't have to remember most of it. She told me to write it down. She said the last time she had ordered, the market had left off several items, and she didn't want it to happen again. She practically shouted at me!"

' "Where are the notes?"

"Here."

Carter took the pad and stared at the page.

"Vietnamese. I write it faster than English."

Carter was patient. "Okay, translate, and fill in what isn't written down."

Lin threw her head back, concentrated for a moment, and then started.

"She said that she and the doctor had unexpected guests. They will need the order very quickly. Then she gave me the list of groceries."

Carter listened to the long list, and as he did so, he felt the fatigue draining from his body and his muscles relaxing.

Patrice Falkner was quite a lady, very sharp.

Komuku had evidently taken Soo Lee to the doctor's residence, and somehow Patrice had been able to speak to her.

Though the list was long, the amount number of each item was the same down the line: eleven chickens, five pounds of raw rice, eleven heads of cabbage, five bunches of asparagus, eleven small sacks of walnuts, five sheets of diced pork . . . and so on.

Carter could only guess, but he would lay even money he was right.

Eleven . . . N11 . . . Soo Lee Culpepper.

"Five, only five, no more," Patrice had said.

Five could be everyone in the house, or it could be Komuku and four of Connie Chu's people he had recruited at the last minute.

Carter guessed the latter.

"Okay, Lin, what else?"

"Three times she told me exactly what gate to use to come into the grounds. And three times she told me to come to the kitchen entrance, not the servants' entrance. She really stressed that . . . 'Don't come to the servants' entrance,' she said, 'the servants have been sent home.' She would be doing the cooking herself, and she wanted the food brought directly to the kitchen.''

"Good, Lin, absolutely terrific. Now here is what I want you to do. You have Patrice's number?''

"Yes.''

Carter reached for the phone as he explained.

Lin Duong dialed with a shaking finger, then held the phone slightly away from her ear so anything from the other end could be heard by Carter.

"Falkner residence.''

Lin swallowed hard, and Carter slid an arm around her frail shoulders.

There was no mistake. The voice on the phone belonged to Ishi Komuku.

"Uh, Missy Falkener, please.''

"Who is calling?''

"This Wong Chow Market. Missy Falkener, she call for order earlier.''

"Yes, what about it?''

"All trucks out now. Cannot deliver until maybe eight o'clock this evening. That be all right with Missy Falkener?''

"Yes, that will be fine.''

"Thank you so much. Good-bye.''

The girl's hand was shaking so badly that Carter had to replace the receiver himself.

"All right?''

"Perfect,'' he declared, already dialing. "Sip some more brandy. We'll take it from here, and Patrice will be fine. Commander Jarvis, please, Carter calling.''

"Jarvis here.'' It didn't take ten seconds. "We've got no word on the girl.''

"I do, and I've got a way in. I want you to phone up a place called Wong Chow Market and apply a little muscle. Talk only to the owner, and here's how you handle it . . .''

This time Jarvis didn't argue. He agreed to the whole plan and had the perfect men who could pose as drivers.

"One more thing, Commander. Given the time, how long will it take for your people to crack those crates safely, and without destroying what's inside?"

"Twenty-four hours, give or take."

"And can they be resealed?"

"Hard to say. We have the equipment to do it. It just depends how much damage is necessary to get them open."

"We'll take that chance. Go to work on them!"

"Will do."

Then Carter made what he hoped would be the last call of the day. A man answered.

"Chu residence. Who calls?"

"Miss Chu is expecting my call."

When she answered, her voice was like syrup.

"Nick, you're five minutes early."

"An old habit of mine."

"Well?"

"It's a deal . . . on my terms."

"I'll listen," she replied.

"Command Center at your place. I'll be there at midnight. We'll make the trade at one in the morning, you on one phone to your people, me on another with mine."

"Sounds good so far."

"I'll have the crates in a van on Hollywood Road, in front of the Man Mo Temple. Where do I get the woman?"

"Hold on . . ."

It was just that, a click, and he was on hold.

"Are you still there?"

"Of course I'm still here, breathless."

She chuckled. "You're such a charmer. It's a pity it has to be like this, Nick, but . . ."

"I know, a girl has to make a living. Save it. Where!"

"Repulse Bay. She'll be tied up on one of the fishing boats anchored in the bay. Send your people to Pie How's hut, in the Chinese market. Our man there will tell you which boat."

Clever, Carter thought, *very clever. A place where, if*

everything doesn't go well, they can take her clear out into the China Sea for burial.

"Agreed?"

"It's agreed," Carter replied. "I'll see you tonight."

"Chivas, wasn't it? . . . One cube?"

"That's right."

"I'll have it waiting."

Carter dropped the phone to its cradle, lit a cigarette, and settled back with a sigh.

"Mr. Carter . . .?"

He looked up. She was fairly calm now, and most of the redness was gone from her eyes.

"Yes?"

"Thank you."

"Don't thank me yet, darlin'," he replied. "It's going to be a long night."

TWELVE

The house was in an exclusive residential area on the Shanghai Road, just before slipping out of Kowloon proper and into the New Territories.

The mansion was left over from the colonial age. It was big, impressive, stark white, and had a high wrought-iron fence covering its entire perimeter.

Carter, with Giles Gordon at the wheel, did three drive-bys in an unmarked sedan.

"Looks like the garage was an old stable, set away from the main house like that."

Carter nodded, his eyes giving his mind the pictures needed to piece together the approach.

Once through the front gate, the drive split; one way led up to the huge front veranda of the house, the other all the way around to the rear. Once there, it broke off and made its return swing around the garage and headed back to the main gate.

On both sides of the drive, house, and garage, hibiscus and oleander grew as thickly as weeds, and this time of year they were in full bloom.

"Chances are the servants' entrance is on that side of the house, just short of the rear."

Gordon agreed. "That would fit with the layout of most of these old mansions. In the old days, it was easier for a horse-drawn carriage to unload there, and it would also give the servants easy access to the stables and the outside cookhouse."

"I'll have the boys drive to the back and unload. Then I'll say bye-bye when they make the turn around the garage. It's ten-to-one Komuku's people are only watching the gate and the drive."

"I'd say you're right."

"Okay, let's get back to the van."

It was a white, made-over Land-Rover, parked about a mile away on Jordan Road.

Carter laid out the plan to the two Chinese MI6 agents, then crawled into the jammed rear of the van.

There were cartons of groceries ceiling high, with the Falkner order near the rear door. The rest had been arranged so that they would provide a cubbyhole in the center to hide Carter's big body.

"All set, Mr. Carter?"

"Ready to roll!"

Then they were moving.

Carter checked the dual loads in the sawed-off Webley shotgun and reslung the lethal piece over his shoulder.

There was no need to check the Luger nestled under his left armpit. He had cleaned it and pumped in a fresh magazine before leaving Patrice Falkner's bungalow that afternoon.

Lin Duong was packed and already at the airport. If all went well, one of Jarvis's men would be driving Pat Falkner to join her in less than two hours.

It was the least Carter could do for the woman, and, also, he wanted everyone out of the country before the real big one with Charlie Loo finally came down.

The van started to slow. Carter craned his neck upward

from his hole. Through a piece of the windshield, he saw the gate and the impressive stone mansion beyond.

"Yes?" came a muffled voice from the intercom that connected the gate to the house.

"Delivery . . . Wong Chow Market."

There was no reply, but the last thing Carter saw before he ducked his head back down was the two big gates swinging lazily and quietly inward.

He felt the turn as the van edged around the corner of the house into the rear courtyard near the kitchen entrance.

"Right there is fine!"

It was a gruff voice, male. Carter didn't recognize it. But then he didn't expect to; Ishi Komuku wouldn't stoop so low as to oversee the unloading of groceries.

He heard rather than saw the white-coated MI6 men slip out of the cab. A few seconds later, the rear doors of the van were thrown wide and the unloading began.

Through a tiny crack between the cartons, Carter could see them in the glare of the courtyard's harsh night floods.

It took about fifteen minutes, and then the doors closed again. One of the men crawled into the passenger side of the van. The other remained at the rear of the vehicle.

"You sign, please?"

"Yes," came the reply, and with a cackling laugh the voice added, "I will sign."

A hand snaked through the cartons with a length of line. Carter took it.

"See any of them?" he whispered.

"Yes," came the reply. "Two Chinese helped unload the groceries. There were two Indian-looking types up on the rear veranda. No hardware showing. They were carrying under their coats, no doubt of it."

"Good enough. See you."

"Good luck!"

Carter moved the cartons aside and made his way to the rear of the van as the driver got in.

He quickly attached the line to the inside handle of one of the doors. When the time came, the line would serve two purposes. One, it was the way he would be signaled to exit. Two, it would give the MI6 man a way to close the rear door after Carter's departure.

The van eased forward, and Carter tensed his body into a crouch on the balls of his feet with his knees near his chest.

There was a slight weight shift as the van started its turn around the garage, and light diminished beyond the cracks around the van's doors.

Keeping one hand on the line, Carter unslung the Webley and cradled it under his right armpit.

The line tensed, went slack, and tensed again. All in one move, Carter cranked the handle, pushed, and catapulted himself into the humid night air.

He lit on his feet, tucked, and, in a ball, rolled to his right under a tall, thick oleander hedge and into a group of dwarf fruit trees beyond.

When he came up in a crouch, the business end of the Webley was raking from the front to the rear of the garage.

Nothing.

He came out of the trees in a crouched run, and made it to the corner of the garage before pausing.

From the rear of the house, probably through an open window, he heard snatches of conversation and male laughter.

But there were no bodies in sight.

Directly across from where he crouched, twenty yards away, was the plain, stained wood door of the servants' entrance.

Cautiously, he peered around the corner of the garage and scanned the manicured gardens beyond the rear courtyard. Nothing, and no one that he could see in the front.

He took a deep breath and literally plunged forward, his running body on a slant. He barely paused at the door, wrenching it open and shoving the snout of the Webley in first.

It was a small hallway, lit by a lone small-watt bulb in a sconce above his head. There were three doors: left, right, and dead center in front of him.

A crack in the left one revealed an empty, high-ceilinged parlor. He edged forward and checked out the center door. It led to the dining room and, from the sound, to the kitchen beyond.

Just as he guessed, the remaining door revealed a narrow set of stairs. He was sure they would lead directly up to the servants' sleeping quarters, probably in the garrets of the fourth floor he had seen from the street.

The climb was quick and, because of the soft-soled deck shoes he wore, silent. At the top he cautiously opened a second door.

The landing was well lighted by a ceiling fixture, and from the banister he could see all the way down the stairwell to the ground floor.

Like a statue he stood, frozen, his ears attuned to every sound. The only rumble still seemed to be coming from the kitchen—at least from the first floor. He could detect no sound at all on the second or third floors.

Behind him, the door to the servants' corridor was open. He could see narrow strips of light under two doors far down toward the end.

He debated. Was it best to check out these rooms first? If someone were behind those doors, he could be flanked when all hell busted out down below.

He decided to risk it and moved to the stairs. Step by step, he soundlessly descended to the third floor landing.

There were five doors in the corridor. Two close, two near the very front flanking a huge bay window overlooking Shanghai Road. The fifth door was far less ornate than the other four. He guessed a utility closet. Light seeped from the far right-hand door.

As Carter moved forward, he tensed the muscle in his right forearm, shooting Hugo's warm hilt into his palm. Just as he was reaching for the knob, he heard the muffled flush of a toilet. The sound was quickly followed by what sounded like the *tap-tap-tap* of sharp female heels.

He took no chances and moved to the side of the door, flattening his back against the wall.

Patrice Falkner opened her mouth to scream when she saw the pencil-thin blade of the stiletto poised just under her right nostril.

At the same instant, she looked beyond the stiletto and saw Carter's smiling face.

It was as if bone, marrow, and muscle oozed from her body in that same instant.

Her knees turned to water and she sagged forward.

Carter quickly moved the stiletto aside and caught her in the crook of his right arm.

"Dear God," she groaned, "you scared me to death!"

"Shhh!" he hissed. "You were expecting me."

"Not really. I was only hoping. Lin sounded so confused on the telephone."

"Well, it worked. You're a very ingenious lady. Where is she?"

"Second floor," she replied. "The same room location as this."

She inclined her head back into the room she had just exited, and Carter nodded. "All right. Is there a bathroom near the back door?"

She nodded. "Just off the kitchen."

"Good. Get down there fast, and lock yourself in. Don't come out for anything, no matter how much hell you hear being raised. If it works, I'll come for you that way. Don't open the door until you hear my voice. Now move!"

Her legs were still shaky, but she managed to reach the

stairwell, and then Carter followed her down with his eyes. He waited until he was fairly sure she had hit the first floor, and then he started moving himself. Just short of the stairs, he heard a door slam in the servants' quarters above him.

"Son of a bitch," he growled under his breath, knowing that he had made a mistake by not checking the lights under those doors. Hurriedly, he found the light switch and snapped it off, leaving the landing in darkness. The only light came up from the floor below.

Just as Carter stepped back into the corridor, he heard footfalls descending the stairs. The first thing he saw was the ugly snout of a submachine gun. It was quickly followed by a short, stout Chinese man, completely dressed in black from head to toe.

Quickly, he analyzed his options: let the man go on, or kill one of the birds in the bush while he had him.

The decision was made for him.

When the man reached the landing, instead of going on down to the second floor, he turned into the corridor and came face to face with Carter.

Just as his eyes grew wide, Carter snapped on the bright overhead light, temporarily blinding him. At the same time, he brought the barrel of the Webley down across the man's wrist. Just as the submachine gun made a muffled thud hitting the thick carpet, Carter flipped Hugo around and thrust the deadly blade smoothly between the man's ribs.

There was no sound as the body slipped to the floor.

The Killmaster slung the Webley back over his shoulder, grabbed the man by the belt with one hand, and picked the hardware from the carpet with the other. In five swift tugging strides, he had backpedaled to the room with the open door and thrust the body inside. He unclipped the magazine from the sub, pocketed it, and headed for the second floor.

He moved on across the landing, killing the light as he passed. At the door he paused, his ears straining for any sound on the other side. There wasn't any, but he was sure the girl would not be left unguarded. He made a fist and lightly rapped on the door.

There was a grunting reply, and Carter replied in kind, muffling his voice with his arm. "Tea for you."

He could hear no sound from within the room, but a few seconds later there was a soft footfall and the bolt slid back. Slowly the door began to open.

Carter had taken a pace backward, and the second that light came through, he hurled himself forward. His shoulder struck the door solidly, slamming it against the guard and spinning him around. The man fell backward on stumbling feet, and Carter was on him in an instant.

He hit the man gut-high with his shoulder and came down on top of him. He was just bringing the barrel of the Webley down across the man's head, when two powerful hands grasped his wrist.

Like Hugo's victim, this one was short, squat, and as strong as an ox. In a microsecond, he had recovered from the surprise of the attack and twisted the Webley around until the barrel was heading toward Carter's shoulder. At the same time, he had gripped Carter's fingers on the trigger and was applying pressure.

Inexorably, the gun was being twisted to bear on him, and Carter knew that in a second or two there would be enough pressure exerted on his trigger finger to fire. Hugo was still in his right hand.

Carter did the only thing possible. Again he flipped the knife, point down, and fell on the hilt with his chest. The blade sank to its hilt in the struggling man's throat, and instantly a flood of blood cascaded from the wound.

But with his dying breath, the man forced Carter's finger down on the Webley's trigger. The roar of the exploding shotgun was like a mortar going off in the otherwise quiet room.

Instantly, Carter's ears rang with the sound, so he could

not hear the shattering of a nearby lamp. But he could see the ornate pedestal and lampshade explode. He rolled from the man beneath him and shook his head to clear it. He could already hear pounding feet on the carpeted stairs.

There was nothing else to do. Quickly, he unlocked the Webley, shoved two fresh shells into the chambers, felt rather than heard the click as he locked it up, and waited.

The first man through the door was one of the Indians.

He was dapper, wearing a dark silk jacket with a deep red cravat at the neck. His eyes, behind half-moon glasses, were wide and looking everywhere when he hit the door.

They grew even wider as Carter pumped one load of buckshot dead center in his chest. It lifted him a foot from the floor and slammed him into a second figure in the corridor. The bodies tangled together as they hit the floor, and Carter came to his feet. Just before slamming the door, he fired the second chamber of the Webley, hoping to catch both of them.

When the door was slammed and securely locked, he whirled and leaned against it, surveying the room.

Soo Lee was on the bed, half in and half out of a wrinkled and torn print dress. Her hair and face was a mess, and there was a vacant, unseeing look in her wide, staring eyes.

"Shit," Carter hissed, recognizing the look only too well.

She had been drugged, and heavily.

So much, he thought, for her mobility.

There was a phone on the bedside stand. He lifted the receiver and sighed with relief.

The line was dead.

Jarvis's boys were doing their job.

A heavy door slamming and excited voices brought him back to the matter at hand.

Komuku, the doctor, and the guards that were left couldn't get out. Gordon and Jarvis would have men all around the place by now.

By the same token, Carter couldn't get out with Soo Lee, particularly in the state she was in.

A quick look out the window told him that there was no escape in that direction.

It had to be the hall.

Cautiously, he slid the bolt back and cracked the door an inch.

Both bodies were bloody and still. The second chamber of the Webley had done its duty.

Gambling, Carter stuck his arm and the Webley into the hall.

Nothing.

A quick look confirmed it.

Komuku and the others were waiting for him on the first landing. Why not? It would be a lot easier than charging up the stairs and exposing themselves to the same fate Carter had already meted out to the two hardening stiffs in the corridor.

But there might be another way.

He discarded the Webley, and cleaned and resheathed Hugo. Then he filled his right hand with Wilhelmina and went to the bed.

Gathering Soo Lee into his arms, he entered the corridor. Her flesh was clammy, without any of the warmth of the living. Her eyes were open, staring directly into his face, but he knew she saw nothing. She had been pumped so full of drugs that she had no comprehension of what was going on.

Perhaps, he thought, it was better that way.

She was no more than a feather in his arms as he moved down the corridor toward the landing.

It was deadly silent below now, as Carter tensed his body at the landing. He stayed far back in the shadows, expecting a fusillade of gunfire on general principles, if nothing else.

At the turn, he flattened his back against the wall and started up. There was a good chance they had sent a man on up to the third floor, or even the servants' quarters, but he would have to chance it.

Just below the level of the third-floor landing, he set Soo Lee down and carefully raised his head.

Empty.

So far, so good.

He grabbed her, and darted up onto the landing and into one of the rear rooms. Just as he was shutting the door, he heard a shout from below.

"He's not here and the woman is gone!"

There had been another way into the room where Soo Lee had been held, and Carter had missed it. That was why they hadn't bothered to mount a frontal attack from the corridor; they figured they could surprise him.

Unceremoniously, he dropped Soo Lee on the bed and opened one of the rear windows as far as it would go. An outcropping of the roof blocked the window from the court-yard, and a huge, old-style, roof-mounted air-conditioning unit screened much of it from the street.

Quickly, he shredded the sheets on the bed and several more from a nearby closet. When the strips were tied to-gether, he rigged a sling in one end and slipped it under the doped woman's arms.

When he was sure it was secure enough to hold her weight, he tied the other end to a drainpipe and began lowering her. When he ran out of length, he leaned far out the window to check.

She swung gently back and forth about twenty-five feet from the ground in a shadowed depression between the out-cropping walls of the front and rear bedrooms.

Carter smiled. Even if they got him, they would have one hell of a time finding her.

He knew he could shout for Jarvis's men, but if they came in blazing, there was no way Connie Chu wouldn't hear about it. And that was the last thing Carter wanted.

Besides, visions of Fancy Adams's mutilated body still flickered on the back of his eyelids.

He wanted Ishi Komuku for himself.

Once the bolt was slid open on the door, he returned to the window. He slid, feet first, through the opening and probed until he could find solid footing. Once this was done, he closed the window and jiggled both sides until the lift-lock fell into place.

Then he started up.

Halfway across the roof toward the front of the house, he could make out sounds from below. They were doing a room-to-room, trying to flush him out.

As he moved, he did a body count. There were three down. Patrice had said five. That meant Komuku, one guard, and maybe the doctor.

Carter doubted if Dr. Falkner was the type who would give him any trouble.

He had passed the garretted turrets of the servants' quarters and reached the front of the roof, when a window flew open behind him and to his right.

He heard no sound, but from the corner of his eye he saw orange flame split the darkness just as a slug tore into the soft tar of the roof near his feet.

He whirled, bringing up Wilhelmina.

The man was leaning far out the window, and Carter could see the glint of moonlight on the gun he held.

He got off one more wild shot as Carter fired.

The figure in the window jerked spastically, toppled forward, and fell with a sickening thud to the unyielding cement of the courtyard below.

Carter didn't pause. His original plan had been to get down by using one of the drainpipes at the front of the house. But Komuku would now know that his last man had fallen. If Carter guessed right about the little assassin, he didn't like even odds.

He ran to the rear of the house and checked. The pool was off one corner, at the rear edge of the courtyard about twenty yards from the house.

He backed off to the middle of the roof, dug in, and ran. He came off the edge of the roof, flat out. In the air, he tucked into a ball and rolled out of it feet first.

Halfway down, he knew he was going to make it with five feet to spare.

Just before he hit, he gently lobbed Wilhelmina toward a grassy patch of ground at the pool's edge.

He hit, went under, and pushed back to the surface in seconds.

His head had barely cleared the water when he heard a scream from the rear of the house. He was just scrambling to the edge of the pool, when Komuku slammed through the rear door. There was a dazed look on his face when he saw Carter. Then there was another scream, and Komuku whirled.

It was then that Carter saw the reason for the look and the staggering way the man moved.

The hilt of a ten-inch bread knife was protruding from high in the man's back.

Carter found Wilhelmina, but he had no need for firepower.

Patrice Falkner came out the rear door, a Webley .45 blazing in her hands. She was unloading the full seven-shot magazine in the general direction of Komuku as she walked.

Not all the slugs found their mark, but enough did to topple the Japanese backward into the pool.

He floated facedown, an ever-widening dark blotch thickening the water around him.

Carter was at Patrice's side in seconds, lifting the automatic from her hands.

"The doctor?"

She nodded, and Carter raced for the house.

He could guess what had occurred.

Patrice couldn't stand it. She had left the bathroom. The light was still on and the door was open.

Bruno Falkner was sitting at the kitchen table. In the process of cutting the doctor's throat, Komuku must have set the Webley on the table.

Patrice saw what he was doing, or had already done. The

wooden rack and the rest of the knives were scattered on the floor.

But the bread knife in the back hadn't killed Komuku, so she had grabbed the Webley.

There was no rush now. Carter lit a cigarette as he walked out the front door and down the drive to summon Commander Jarvis.

He hoped the commander had a very good garbage crew. It would be a long night's work cleaning up this mess.

He checked his watch. It was eleven o'clock.

See you in an hour, Connie Chu.

THIRTEEN

The house was modern, but between color and touches of architectural details on the doors and along the roof line, it had suggestions of old China. Like the house of the recently deceased Dr. Bruno Falkner, there was a tall fence all around the grounds.

The two men on the gate were hard types, but they became extremely polite when Carter identified himself.

He left the car directly in front of the door and mounted four marble steps intricately inlaid with colorful chips of polished glass.

Carter was calm, almost peaceful, like the night around him.

What a change, he thought, from an hour before.

Jarvis had solemnly taken command. Soo Lee had been lowered to the ground and immediately rushed to a hospital. After a brief interrogation, Patrice Falkner had been driven to Kai Tak Airport.

And then the garbage crew had gone to work.

Oddly enough, and at this Carter smiled, there had not been one report to the police about the disturbance.

A rule of thumb in Hong Kong: Live and let live.

The front door was a massive thing, with brass fittings and ten layers of glossy red shellac. He punched the bell, and from somewhere on the other side of the door a few muted Chinese gongs announced his arrival.

It opened immediately.

"Good evening, Mr. Carter. Madame Chu awaits you on the rear terrace. Will you follow me, please?"

He had the perfect manners and the precise elocution of a good valet or butler, but he had the sinewy grace and light step of a martial arts master.

He also had very efficient eyes. They had scanned Carter's body and in seconds spotted the bulge of Wilhelmina's shoulder rig under his left armpit.

They passed through a sitting room, all cool stone surrounded by hanging tapestries and thick Oriental throw rugs. The open beams and other wood in the eighteen-foot-high ceiling had been shellacked like the door.

The house, thus far, oozed the hot and cold, yet impersonal, personality of its owner.

Her man opened a tall French door, and Carter stepped out onto the terrace.

"Good evening, Nicholas."

She was sitting at a table, away from the light. A drink tray was at her elbow, and two telephones rested on the low, round table before her.

Carter suppressed a sigh of relief. There were no loose ends. No one had called and informed her that he was now playing with a stacked deck and she held a dead hand.

As he sauntered forward, she plucked a drink from the tray, stood, and oozed her way toward him.

"Chivas, one cube."

"Your memory is as well preserved as the rest of you." He took the drink and sipped, studying Connie Chu's porcelain features over the rim of the glass.

Her laughter was husky. It could only be called jaded, like

her dark, brooding eyes and her cruel, thin lips. "You haven't changed, either, Nicholas . . . other than that horrible haircut."

"It used to be a shave. May we sit? I've had a long evening."

"Of course."

He watched her move like a graceful jungle cat back to her chair. She was wearing pure white, with no accessories to mar the stark look. The silk dress clung like wet gauze to every hill and hollow of her still glorious body.

Her high, taut breasts pushed themselves against the restraining material as if it were a personal insult to them. Her movement was pure undulation, a study in female locomotion, as she slid into the chair.

"I thought you might at least kiss me," she cooed, crossing her legs so that the two halves of the cheongsam parted.

"Later . . . perhaps." He slid into the opposite chair and produced his cigarette case. "Are your people in place?"

"Of course. And yours?"

Carter nodded. "How many guns do you have up here, besides the butler and the two on the gate?"

She shrugged. "That's all. I don't need any more than those three. They are all experts."

"I'm sure they are. Send the two on the gate away."

"What?"

"I said, send the two on the gate down the hill. Tell them to get a beer or get laid, I don't care. I want the odds a little more even after our trade is completed."

The already narrow eyes slitted further, and Carter could almost hear the tumblers clicking in her well-honed brain.

At last she shrugged and raised one finger from around her glass.

"Yes, madam?"

Carter tensed. The butler had appeared on cat feet and out of nowhere. He would have to remember that when the time came.

Connie Chu barked a long phrase in Cantonese, and the man disappeared.

Carter looked around. "Business has been good lately."

"It was never bad," she countered. "There are too many greedy people in the world that keep it that way."

"Why Charlie Loo?"

"Why not? It was a perfect setup and fit in with the rest of my operation. All I had to do was pass along a small package and lend a few hands to Ishi when they were needed."

"Then Komuku *is* the main man down here?"

She nodded. "He and Charlie are very close . . . you might say related, in a way. Ishi's sister is Charlie's mistress."

"Just one, big, happy family." Carter finished his drink.

"Another?"

He shook his head. "One's my limit when I'm working. Is your butler as good as Komuku?"

"Better, perhaps. Why?"

Carter smiled. "Just wondering how much effort I'll have to exert in killing him."

That got her. The almost liquid slouch disappeared from her body. The legs uncrossed, and as she leaned forward, the knuckles around her glass contrasted sharply with the crimson color of her long nails.

"I hope you're not planning on silly games tonight, Nicholas. You are a very dangerous man, but I must tell you, I fear Charlie Loo far more than I fear you."

"You won't have to much longer. I plan on eliminating Charlie Loo . . . with your help."

There was no humor in the way she threw back her beautiful head and let a rippling laugh curl up the long column of her throat.

"To kill Charlie Loo, Nicholas, you will have to find him. Believe me, that is impossible."

Carter finally lit the cigarette he had been rolling between his fingers. He took a too-deep drag and let the smoke burn the far depths of his lungs before exhaling.

"I believe you when you say Charlie Loo has a very deep hole. He is too smart not to, considering he's wanted in about five countries. Komuku was probably the only person who knew Charlie's location and how to get to him. But I think, Connie Chu, that *you* know how to get in touch with Charlie."

Her smooth forehead puckered into a frown. She was dissecting his every word.

And then she had it. Carter could see the flashbulbs going off in those coal black pupils.

"You said 'was' when you spoke of Ishi . . ."

"He's dead. About an hour ago, at the Falkner place. Bruno Falkner also bought it, along with all your people. Everything's over, Madame Chu."

"That's impossible!"

"Is it? Johannson's alive. He'll testify in return for immunity. I've got the crates, and we'll get them open. It's over, at least for you, Connie. I might miss Charlie . . . this time . . . but I'm going to get you."

The movement was so slight, this time with only a pinky finger, that had Carter glanced away for a fraction of a second, he would have missed it.

As it was, the finger was barely coming up when Carter rolled out of the chair. The release spring shot Hugo into his palm like a striking snake.

The butler was five feet behind Carter's chair, a silenced .38 raised in both hands. Out of the corner of his eye, the Killmaster saw the cushion, where his back had been recently resting, explode.

It was all done in one, smooth, fluid motion. His knee hit the deck of the terrace, his arm swung up in a smooth arc, the wrist releasing the stiletto at just the right instant.

He wanted a neck, a windpipe if possible, but missed by

four inches. The blade entered just under the left collarbone, far from a kill but more than enough to bring a scream of pain from the man and divide his concentration.

Carter was a leaping blur right behind Hugo. Before his prey could bring the .38 around for another shot, Carter was halfway by him.

The butler tried to turn and follow, but Carter pirouetted, came to the very tip of his toes, and brought the calloused side of his hand down across the man's neck. The Killmaster heard, as well as felt, several vertebrae give and break.

He could have left it at that, but he knew a point had to be made. A sideways glance at Connie Chu confirmed it. She was desperately trying to dig a tiny .22 peashooter from between the cushions of the settee.

Carter held up the partially unconscious but still howling-in-pain man, and waited until she had the gun clear and up in both hands.

Their eyes met and then, almost in slow motion, the Killmaster moved.

He wrapped his right arm around the other's neck until the point of the chin was cradled in his elbow. Then, using his own left elbow as a fulcrum off his right hand, Carter placed his left palm forward at the back of the man's head.

Carter knew Connie Chu. She was evil to the core of her beautiful body. She had absolutely no compunctions about ordering the death of one or ten men.

But in her case, "ordering" was the operative word. She hated to get her own hands dirty, and at her very core was a squeamishness born of the fear that in the midst of violence, she herself could be harmed.

Carter lifted his knee into the small of the man's back. There was a quick lift, a hard twist, and the snap of the spine was like a muffled rifle shot across the terrace.

Connie Chu's eyes grew wide and her body began to shake. The peashooter in her hands wavered, but she finally managed to squeeze off one, and then a second shot as Carter advanced.

Both slugs thudded harmlessly into the already very dead body just before Carter unceremoniously draped the corpse over Connie Chu's screaming face.

With two fingers, he picked the gun from her hand and carelessly tossed it over the side of the terrace. He slid his right hand under his jacket, unsheathed the Luger, and stepped back to watch the woman wriggle from beneath the bloody body of her servant.

When she did, Carter stepped forward again and touched the tip of her nose with the Luger's ugly snout.

"Lie still and listen!"

She made no sound, and her dark eyes were nearly crossed gazing at the Luger.

"Are you listening?" He flipped the safety off and pushed a little.

She nodded.

"I didn't hear you!"

"I . . . I'm listening, goddamn you!"

"Good. You're done, Madame Chu. But I want Charlie Loo. I want you to get in touch with him. Hear me?"

"I hear you."

"I'm giving you a second chance to save your beautiful, miserable skin. I want you to tell Charlie that you got the goods, both crates. Tell him that Komuku and Falkner bought it, but your people were able to make the trade. There will be backup stories in tomorrow's Hong Kong papers, not enough to say everything, but enough to convince Charlie that he can get his gold mine back. Now, what do you think he'll do?"

She didn't have to think very long. "He'll come after them himself."

"That's right, because he doesn't have anybody left down here he can trust. Now, when he's taken the bait, here's how we snap the trap shut.''

With Wilhelmina's muzzle still tickling her nose, Carter explained in intricate detail just what he wanted her to say and how she should react to what Charlie Loo would say.

It took about ten minutes, and by the end of it she had regained much of her composure.

''Would you mind taking that thing away from my face? It's obvious you're not going to shoot me.''

''Sure.''

Carter slid the Luger home and casually poured himself another drink.

''What's in it for me?'' she asked, pulling herself to her feet.

Carter smiled around the rim of his glass. She was hooked.

''If I get Charlie Loo, I really don't give a damn about you. You've still got your money and your junks. One of these days you'll trip, and the locals will take you down. No skin off my nose.''

The sudden glaze in her eyes and the smirk that spread across her thin lips told him her thoughts better than words: *Fat chance of that!*

''I'll do it.''

''I knew you would. Now you'd better go take a shower and change before we make the call. You're a bloody mess . . . *his* blood.''

She looked down, gasped, and hurried away with one hand over her mouth and one over her stomach.

Carter smiled again.

Whatever Connie Chu had eaten for dinner was about to be lost.

FOURTEEN

Deep Water and Repulse actually made up one bay, with the peninsulas of Stanley on one side and Ocean Park on the other. There were a few small islands in the center that separated the bays.

These would be a bit of a problem, but Carter was counting on the beeper device he had planted in Connie Chu's cosmetic bag to tell them where she was at all times.

Hopefully, for the next few hours, Connie would be in the same place as Charlie Loo.

It had taken three phone calls to Japan from her villa to get through the security screen Charlie had set up.

Out of greed, and her newfound fear of Carter, Connie had played her part well.

Komuku and four of her people were dead, but she had the crates. What did he want her to do?

Were the crates still sealed?

Yes.

He would call her back.

The twenty-four-hour-wait had seemed interminable. In that time, Carter had huddled intensely with Commander Jarvis and Giles Gordon. If Charlie Loo took the bait and came out of his hole to handle this tricky situation in person, there was no way of knowing how he would arrive. They had to plan for every contingency by sea, by air, even by land.

Carter was fairly sure Charlie Loo had the contacts to come right down from mainland China if he so desired.

Soo Lee Culpepper had been released from the hospital with a clean bill of health.

She wanted in on the kill. Because of what she had gone through, Carter didn't have the heart to deny her.

At last, a second call came.

Was Connie Chu positive that Carter and British intelligence hadn't connected her?

She was positive. Komuku had killed Dr. Falkner before any connection to her was revealed.

On the phone, Charlie Loo sounded convinced, but he had told Connie to wait for yet another message.

More pacing, more cigarettes, and more booze to soften the agony of waiting. Soo Lee had spent the night with Carter, but both of them had been so tense that they hadn't even touched each other.

They could just as well have had a bundling board in the bed.

"Later, when this is over," Carter had said.

"I agree. We'll rent a boat. I have this little house on this little island . . ."

They hardly slept.

Then, at ten the previous evening, Charlie Loo had called again . . . from somewhere in the Hong Kong area.

"Jesus Christ," Carter had groused at Giles Gordon, "he's in! How the hell did he do it?"

"One of five hundred ways," Gordon had sighed. "An elephant could slip into Hong Kong or the New Territories undetected if it had the right connections."

Charlie Loo's directions were specific. Connie Chu was to drive immediately to the south of the island and check into the Repulse Bay Hotel. At precisely nine the next morning,

she was to check out of the hotel—with *all* of her luggage—
and go to the pier.

There she was to wait.

It was a good plan. At that hour of the morning, the bay
would be jammed with boats and the wide, sandy beaches
would be highly populated with sunbathers.

By the same token, Charlie Loo could have a car stashed
somewhere close by. Repulse Bay Boulevard would be
clogged to the gills with traffic. He could transfer the cases
and make a land run for it.

"I don't think so," Giles had offered. "If he's got a real
fast boat, he could make any one of a dozen islands. Also, he
could head up here, to Aberdeen, and lose himself among the
boat people. There's an entire city up there on the water, and
if we tried to take him, it's no telling how many people he
would take with him."

They came up with the most complete plan possible, using
every available man, and then topped it with the crates
themselves.

"They're ready?" Carter had asked.

"Yes. We were able to copy enough to convince the
businessmen in Japan to get out of business, and we put your
surprise packages inside both of them before we resealed
them."

Here Gordon had paused, searching Carter's face with a
haunted vacancy in his eyes.

"What about the Chu woman?"

"What about her?"

"She is helping us. I mean, if you have to use the last
resort . . ."

Carter had shrugged. "She would order the both of us
killed much more quickly than I would push the button on
her."

"You know something, Carter?"

"What?"

"I just realized I don't like us very much."

Now Carter sat behind the wheel of a powerful motor launch. He was idling in an inlet of one of the islands in the center of the bay. Gordon was in another launch near the hotel pier.

On shore, three cars were manned along Repulse Bay Boulevard, and six men were scattered over the hotel grounds, also near the pier.

Their orders were to observe—a hands-off policy—until Charlie Loo's plan of escape became clear.

The idea was to move Charlie Loo into the open before any attempt was made to take him.

As a backup to the whole, Commander Jarvis was freewheeling in a helicopter a few hundred yards out to sea.

For all intents and purposes, Carter knew that everything was covered. But he also knew Charlie Loo.

The man was like a cunning eel. He could slip through anything, and if he were cornered with no escape, he would be like a ferocious rat.

Everything was set to go. But how and where?

Carter didn't really know. He had no sure plan, in fact, except following Charlie Loo once he had the crates and hoping there was a clear opening to take him.

Carter adjusted the radio volume and depressed the button on the mike in his hand.

"Giles . . . Giles, are you there? Over."

"Here, old man. There's a good-sized one coming down around Ocean Point, but it's still too far away to make out any markings. Moving fast, though. Over."

"Keep me up-to-date. Over."

"Will do. Out."

Carter was about to hang up the microphone, when Commander Jarvis's voice broke through the static.

"Carter . . . ?"

"Here, Commander. Go ahead."

"Miss Chu is on the pier, complete with luggage and crates."

"Good. Keep your men fairly close. If he feels safe, he might step off the boat to supervise the loading. Then it's only a question of how many around him."

"Righto."

"Carter—"

It was the other boat. "Go ahead, Gordon."

"That big one's around Ocean Head and coming into the bay—fast! One man, no crew that I can see. It's a beauty . . . twin diesels and no load, riding high in the water."

"Can you make out any markings?"

"Wait a minute . . . yes, it's the *Dragon Master*, out of Macao. It must be Loo . . . he's heading around toward the inlet that borders the hotel!"

"I've got him," Carter said. "Keep me informed when he gets to the pier!"

"Will do. Out."

On the wheel, Carter's palms started to sweat. But it wasn't from fear; it was anticipation. He wanted Charlie Loo. He had missed him once, and come hell or high water, he wasn't going to miss him again.

There was a long wait, and then more static and Gordon's voice.

"Nick . . . ?"

"Here. Go ahead!"

"The bastard's really playing it cozy."

"How so?"

"He's idled down about fifty yards from the pier and hailed a water taxi. The taxi's going in for Chu!"

Cute, Carter thought, *so it's going to be by sea*.

"Tell your boys on the beach to lay back. It's our game now . . . you, me, and the commander."

"Righto. She's aboard the water taxi and they're headed back."

"Did you read all that, Commander?"

"Affirmative. Ready and waiting. Good hunting."

"Here we go!" Carter said. "Out."

He set the mike down and flipped on the portable radar unit. The set hummed, the screen flashed white, and then it settled down to its normal green color with the yellow circling wand. The beep and the little white ball were clear each time the whirling line passed over the spot where Connie Chu was.

Carter smiled. He had guessed right. Connie did indeed carry her cosmetic case wherever she went. The tiny, transistorized beeper inside a tube of lipstick was tuned to a channel on the portable radar screen beside the Killmaster.

As he watched the little white dot move on the screen, the launch's powerful Chrysler marine engine beneath him roared to life.

Charlie Loo kept the powerful engines of the *Dragon Master* idling in reverse as he watched Connie Chu step aboard the yacht from the water taxi.

He was a short, compact man, with powerful shoulders, a thin waist, and narrow hips. His face, as always, held no expression. Only the glint in his marblelike eyes would give away the fact that he was alive.

Now those eyes appraised Connie Chu's body in the silk sheath. It was attractive, but he had already experienced it to the fullest, so there was no craving.

His gaze went on past the woman to the two men in the water taxi. Two expensive bags and a small case came over the side. they were quickly followed by the two crates.

Then and only then did the semblance of a smile spread his thin lips.

The water taxi's driver had barely been paid, when Charlie Loo eased the twin throttles forward and nosed the big boat around toward the center of the bay.

Behind him he could hear the *tap, tap, tap* of Connie Chu's high heels on the deck.

Stupid woman, he thought, *wearing heels aboard a moving boat!*

Then she was in the wheelhouse and moving forward to stand beside him.

"It's been a long time, Charlie. I mean, since we've actually seen each other in person."

Coy bitch, he thought. *Can she actually think I want her for any reason other than to serve as a lacky?*

"Saigon was a long time ago," he replied flatly. "Did you send your junks out as I told you?"

"I did."

And she had. Of course, she hadn't told Carter that sending all her junks to sea in precise patterns and to specific destinations was part of Charlie Loo's orders.

That would be *her* escape valve if Carter didn't kill Loo.

"Is that what we're going to do . . . board one of my junks at sea?"

"Perhaps," he replied, his voice revealing nothing. "I can't be arrested in international waters if you have compromised me, can I?"

"Charlie, I have done everything you said."

She shivered when he turned toward her. His eyes, she thought, could kill with a look.

"In the meantime, we are just out for a leisurely cruise, so why don't you go below and change into something more suitable for cruising?"

"Of course, Charlie."

She tried to kiss him on the cheek, but he turned away.

She tottered from the wheelhouse and, one by one, struggled her bags below.

Charlie Loo set the automatic pilot and went aft to check on the crates. When he was sure that they hadn't been tampered with, he returned to the wheelhouse and brought a pair of powerful binoculars up to his eyes.

Twice he made a 360-degree arc around the bay, his gaze missing nothing.

He could see nothing out of the ordinary, no section of the bay or beach that had been evacuated.

But still there was something wrong. He could feel it, sense it.

And Charlie Loo always followed the dictates of his highly attuned senses.

They had saved him many times from disaster.

Carter idled the launch in shallow water along the rim of the island. Through his own binoculars, he had watched Connie Chu tote her own bags below.

That was good. No crew.

Then he sighed with relief when he watched Charlie Loo inspect the crates and, apparently satisfied, return to the wheelhouse.

If anything would convince him he was safe, it would be the intact condition of the laser locks on the crates. He would know that Carter and company needed the contents of those crates to topple his little house of cards.

They wouldn't be handed over so easily unless they had been rifled. And after checking the crates so carefully, he was obviously sure that had not been done.

When he saw Charlie Loo go to his glasses, Carter darted the launch into an inlet.

It was a waiting game. So far, Charlie Loo hadn't taken any certain direction. After reaching the middle of the bay, the big yacht had arched around and was now slowly idling in a two- or three-hundred-foot circle.

There were smaller boats all around him. It would be impossible to make a clean kill without injuring at least two dozen other people.

Life was cheap in the Orient, but not that cheap. Commander Jarvis had already warned Carter that he would not tolerate another episode like the *Tokyo Star*, even though in that instance no innocent parties had been involved.

"Carter?"

"Yes, Commander?"

"Have you got him?"

"Clear as a bell. I think Gordon is on the other side."

"Good. I'm going to have to move inland a bit. If we stay out here in the copter too long, he'll be sure to smell something."

"All right, Commander. Giles?"

"Here."

"Have you got him?"

"I do. I'm skimming the beach about two hundred meters from him."

"Good. Don't get too tight. I'm going to try to get a closer look from the tip of the island!"

Charlie Loo's suspicions went up two points when he saw the copter swerve inland but remain above the beach.

The beach patrols didn't begin until noon. It was not yet eleven. Then he saw the made-over China patrol boat moving steadily along the beach far too close for fishing. The presence of a second boat—same make, same size—moving out from one of the islands made his skin crawl.

On a hunch, he flipped open the radar panel and began a search with the frequency scanner.

It took him almost ten minutes, but he found it . . . the steady blip. Another ten minutes and he located it . . . right where he was.

He was angry but not shaken. He should have suspected it. Connie Chu's loyalty was only to herself.

The little lady had come aboard with an HF-DF beeper.

He was amused at Carter. The man wanted his kill, Charlie Loo, more than he wanted the crates.

Or perhaps the American agent thought he was good enough to get both.

Just in case, he did a recheck.

Again he switched the HF-DF panel controls on and flipped the dial to "Search."

This time it took a little less than two minutes to zero in on the beeper, and this time he didn't have to go to the grid to locate the source.

Carter had visions of getting close enough to get off a shot with the high-powered sniper rifle in the seat beside him. Even better, if Charlie Loo was lulled into a sense of security, Carter might be able to jump the rail and take the man out with Wilhelmina.

Carter was within twenty yards of the larger craft when he heard the two supercharged diesels rev up.

The *Dragon Master* cut a big, beautiful swath and then headed directly for him. In the wheelhouse, Carter could see Charlie Loo's smiling face.

Gordon's voice came on the radio, screaming through the static: "Carter . . . my God, he's going to ram you!"

Don't you think I know it, Carter's mind roared as he jammed the throttle forward, at the same time spinning the wheel.

He barely avoided the bow of the bigger boat but caught the wake broadside. His stomach threatened to fill his throat as the bow went up, and then farther up. All he could see, for what seemed an eternity, was sky.

Then it came down with a sickening crash, and there was a whirring roar from the stern as the prop lifted out of the water.

The double twisting motion threw Carter up and against the windshield, the top strip of chrome over the windshield hitting him painfully just above his pelvis. Nausea and pain struck at the same time, but he managed to hold on and fall back into the cockpit.

He shook his head from side to side to clear it and frantically clawed the salt water from his eyes. When he could see at last, he found the boat veering in a crazy zigzag pattern and heading toward the rocky coast at full speed.

His hand found the ignition, but too late. Momentum took him clear over one jutting sandbar, and just as the bow crashed into another, the inboard sputtered and died.

Behind him he could see the *Dragon Master*'s huge wake curling five hundred yards out into the bay and rounding Ocean Point.

Charlie Loo rounded Ocean Point and idled down. He eased the *Dragon Master* through a narrow channel and into a tiny private marina.

Two boats bobbed at anchor near a dock, but there wasn't a soul around. Trees shielded the marina from a villa inland about a hundred yards. He would be safe unless someone from the villa decided on a sail. But even that was a minor problem.

He would only be in the marina for a few minutes.

He left the diesels idling and crawled up on the roof of the wheelhouse. With deft hands he went to work on a canvas cover. In minutes it was off, folded, and dropped to the deck below.

He had almost regained the main deck, when Connie Chu stepped out of the hatch.

"My God, Charlie, what the hell is *that*?"

He followed her gaze up to the roof of the wheelhouse and then turned to face her. "That, my dear, is a set of fifty-caliber U.S. Army quad-mounted machine guns."

"Machine . . . ?"

"Connie, would you take your clothes off, please? All of them."

"I certainly will not . . . not up here, at least," she replied coyly.

Loo wound his hand in the front of her dress and, with one powerful yank, tore it and her bra from her body.

"Charlie . . . my God . . . !"

"The shoes, too, Connie," he hissed, shredding first the bra and, finding nothing, going on to the dress. Dumbly, she handed him her shoes as he threw the mangled garments into the water. He ripped the shoes and made her gasp when he cracked them in half with his bare hands.

"A purse, Connie . . . you had a purse when you came aboard. Where is it?"

"Down below," she said weakly, knowing something was now dreadfully wrong. It wasn't going at all as Carter had planned.

He was already past her and going down the ladder. He spotted the purse on the bunk. Dumping its contents, he shredded the bag.

"Jesus Christ, Charlie, that's a Gucci . . ."

"Shut up!" he spat as he went methodically through its contents, ripping and shattering compacts, wallet, and, at last, the lipstick. He withdrew the tiny capsule and held it up to the light streaming through the porthole.

"What the hell is that?"

"That, my dear, is a tiny transmitter," he replied, placing it under his heel and grinding it to pulp. "You've been bugged."

"Bugged . . . but he didn't tell me . . ."

"*Who* didn't tell you . . . Carter?"

"No, Charlie . . . no, I didn't . . ."

Then he turned to face her. It must have been in his eyes, because suddenly she tensed. Her fingers curled into claws. Then, as if she knew she had no chance, she flew at him, scratching at his eyes with her talonlike nails.

Charlie seized her wrists together in one hand and wrenched her hands away from his face as one of her nails gouged a long, deep scratch in his cheek. He smacked her solidly across the mouth with the back of his hand. Her flesh broke under his knuckles as blood burst from her lips and nose.

She gasped with pain and her eyes flooded with tears as the blood gushed down her face. Loo tightened the viselike grip of his left hand over both her wrists and slid his right up between her breasts and over her throat.

"Charlie . . . what's the matter with you? . . . what is

this?'' He squeezed, and her voice became a gagging choke.

"I needed you, Connie, to get inside the bay . . . to get the crates in the open. Now that I've got them, I have no more need of you.''

"I . . . don't . . . understand,'' she rasped. "Charlie . . . please . . . what . . . are you . . . doing . . . ?''

"It's very simple, my dear,'' he replied. "I'm killing you.''

It took almost five precious minutes, with the powerful inboard marine howling at its peak, to backwash the launch's bow off the sandbar.

Carter's heart pounded wildly as he backed around and waited. Was the fiberglass hull shattered? Was he taking on seawater?

He moved the boat gradually into deeper water. The steering was erratic, probably from a gouge below the waterline, but the launch was afloat and mobile.

Quickly his eyes scanned the bay, from Stanley across to the jutting peninsula of Ocean Point. Junks, a few water taxis, but no pleasure boats . . . especially none the class and size of the *Dragon Master*.

Carter throttled up and headed for the mouth of the bay. At the same time, he reached for the hand mike.

"Gordon?''

"Here! I saw. You okay?''

"I think so. Where is he?''

"I lost him around Ocean Point. Carter . . . ?''

"Yeah?''

"I've lost the blip.''

Carter checked his own radar and cursed. His jaw clenched and his lips set in a taut, thin line. "I'll try to flush him out.''

Around the halfway point of the peninsula, toward the landward end, the coastline curved inward. There were about twenty narrow channels leading into private docks and marinas through trees and rugged rocks.

Charlie Loo was in one of them, waiting.

Carter turned the volume back up on the radar unit and checked again.

There was no sound beyond a hum, and there was no tiny green ball disrupting the wand's smooth movement around the screen.

"Sorry, Connie Chu," he murmured under his breath, "but it's a rough game."

Hell to pay now, he hissed to himself. *If Charlie gives up on the crates and runs for cover, he could be lost for good.*

For good, that is, until he comes up with another little scheme!

Carter gunned the launch to full throttle and spun the wheel, sending the boat into the first inlet.

A medium-size pleasure craft was tied up at the dock, and a catamaran bobbed at anchor in the center of the cove.

No *Dragon Master*.

The boat slid around, and Carter was again in open sea. Twice more he performed the same exercise, with the same result.

He was approaching the mouth of the fourth channel, when, above the roar of the launch's inboard, he heard the roar of a more powerful set of engines.

Carter swung his head back to the left just in time to see the bigger boat's sharp bow barreling toward him in the narrow channel.

Instead of turning into the channel, he spun the wheel in the opposite direction.

The launch's momentum was just enough to slide it sideways and away from the *Dragon Master*'s bow.

The larger boat roared by, leaving the launch doing jackrabbit jumps over its wake.

Carter could make out Charlie Loo's figure in the wheelhouse. But it was the equipment on the wheelhouse roof that drew his attention.

For a second the Killmaster held his breath, his mind

willing Charlie Loo to keep the big boat's bow heading toward open sea. If he turned north, toward crowded Aberdeen, the chase would still be on . . . and probably futile.

Then Carter sighed. The *Dragon Master* was plowing straight out into the China Sea.

"You're a dead man, Charlie Loo," Carter muttered, urging every ounce of speed he could from the launch.

As he drove, he reached over and uncapped a small black box beneath the radar system. Wires ran from the box to the launch's powerful generator system. But even as powerful as it was, the detonator in the box would only set off the plastique explosives in the crates from a distance of less than one hundred yards.

Carter would have to stay that close until they were far out to sea.

On and on they raced, and surprisingly, Carter was able to keep up.

And then he got it: a junk on the horizon, the twin .50s on the wheelhouse.

Connie had double-crossed him, and herself at the same time.

Charlie Loo was making for the junk. At the last minute he would idle down, put the yacht on auto, and climb up to the wheelhouse roof.

Then, with the .50s, he would blow any pursuit out of the water.

Sharp. But not sharp enough.

Carter was fifty yards from the yacht when he moved his fingers to the little black box.

He flipped a toggle to "On," and a red button with the word "Fire" in its center lit up.

"So long, Charlie Loo."

Carter swerved the launch hard to port as he depressed the red button.

The *Dragon Master* split in half and became a part of the towering funnel of water caused by the explosion.

Just another accident at sea, Carter mused, not even looking back as he headed for Repulse Bay.

Gray seeped over the horizon as they lay, huddled on a chaise, naked beneath a blanket against the morning chill.

"I like your island."

"Thank you," she said, sliding one leg between his thighs and breathing deeply.

Her breast expanded in his palm, and Carter sighed in contentment.

His reverie was short-lived, interrupted by a jangling phone.

"Must you?" he groaned.

"You do it. Tell them you're the houseboy and we're not here."

Carter slid from beneath the blanket, padded to a nearby table, and lifted the phone.

"Yes?"

There was a crackling of static, and then the familiar voice of David Hawk.

"Well done, Nick, well done! There were seven executives involved. They have all been convinced that resignations are the best way out."

"Fine, sir."

"Terrible connection. Can you hear me all right?"

Carter hesitated for a moment. "Barely, sir."

"Kulo Electronics has been taken over by our people. With any luck, we can plant a man in there to pass some false stuff, maybe negate the damage already done."

"Good idea, sir. It should work."

"Yes. Now, N3, it's good you're where you are. I want you to go down to Singapore. You'll be briefed when you get there. A messy situation. It was just luck that you're already in the area . . ."

Carter glanced over at Soo Lee Culpepper's luscious nude body. The morning breeze wafted across his own body.

It was a lovely setting.

"What's that, sir?"

"I said, I want you to go to Singapore . . ."

"Terrible connection, sir. Tell you what, I'll call you back when it's cleared."

"Nick, can you hear . . . ?"

Carter gently replaced the phone and curled back under the blanket.

"It's typhoon season," Soo Lee said.

"I know. The lines might not be clear for days."

DON'T MISS THE NEXT NEW
NICK CARTER SPY THRILLER

PURSUIT OF THE EAGLE

"Is that you, Max?" the voice called. It was a heavy voice, weighted by authority.

"No, sir!" Carter said in guttural German.

He ran a hand through his dark hair and pulled it into an untidy curtain over his face. He hunched his back so that he was inches shorter.

With his foot, Carter shoved the bucket just outside the door. His gait was rolling, almost crippled, as he walked out.

"Max sent me," Carter said and pushed the bucket.

"Stop that noise!" the voice said irritably. "I can't hear you!"

Carter paused, peered through his curtain of thick hair at a man of medium height with a smooth face and eyebrows so blond that they seemed to disappear against the pale skin.

"Max sent me," Carter repeated, put the rag mop between

the rollers, rotated the handle to squeeze out the water from the cloth head. "Didn't he tell you?"

"Of course not!" the man said, eyes narrowing. A smile of vindictiveness hovered at his mouth. "But he'll wish he had!"

"You'd rather no one cleaned the floors?"

Carter reached into the closet for a box of detergent. The boss man clenched his fists at his sides. Any janitor was better than none. Carter poured the detergent powder into the bucket. The angry man snorted, whirled, and stalked back down the hall.

The agent paused and listened to the disappearing feet ring through the hall. Exuberant laughter and polka music echoed from the beer hall itself.

At last satisfied that he was again alone, Carter stripped off the coveralls and put on his own suit jacket. He walked back to the office and tried the doorknob.

As he'd expected, the door was locked. He glanced again down the hall and saw that it was still empty.

Carter slid the "toothpick" into the door's old-fashioned lock, moved the slender stick around the tumblers. Another of AXE's incredible inventions, the toothpick's computerized electronics rearranged the tumblers with soft clicks.

Carter withdrew the special lock-picker, opened the door, and walked into the dark office. No one would ever know the lock had been picked. He closed the door softly behind him.

The agent slid the toothpick back into its ivory holder, inverted it, pressed the end. A narrow but extremely bright beam of light shot from the holder.

Carter played the light around the room, noted the roll-top desk against one wall, the swivel chair, coffee table, sofa, and three-drawer file cabinet against the wall opposite from the desk.

Quietly Carter walked to the file cabinet.

The office was ordinary, with no marks of distinction to

indicate it was the personal possession of any single human. The only specialness about the plastic and wood interior was a series of framed photographs to the left of the file cabinet.

The photos were dated 1930, 1940, 1950, 1960, 1970, and 1980—photos of the staff of the Bohemian Beer Hall, unconscious records of the aging and mobility of the employees through fifty years.

Invariably, the white-aproned waiters, waitresses, and bartenders were stout with good-natured smiles on their faces and mugs of beer held aloft in their hands. Each decade's group stood before the lattice-framed front door of the Bohemian. The faces differed from photo to photo, but the bodies and assumed smiles didn't—monuments to the changelessness of time.

Carter moved the flashlight to the top file drawer. "A–E," it read. It was locked. Again he inserted the small lock-picker, heard the soft clicks, then opened the drawer.

Ludwig Bretton's file was near the front.

Carter memorized Bretton's appartment address, then read the rest of the file. Bretton was 28, married to Lina Baer, no children. Had played the accordion at the Rhineland for three years, and before that in several beer halls in Munich. He listed his interests as reading and attending dramas such as those at the Schauspielhaus. He said he had only a high school education. Under "aspirations," he'd written "World peace, no matter what the cost." The blanks were filled with writing in the cramped, nearly unreadable scribbles of the mean-spirited and opinionated. Ludwig Bretton promised to be a tenacious adversary.

Carter closed the file, reinserted it in its alphabetical place, and shut the drawer. He ran the toothpick over the tumblers, locking the file drawer again.

As he walked back across the office, he moved the flashlight's strong beam over the furniture, checking once more that he'd disturbed nothing.

It was the sound from the door's hinges and the crack of

light from the hallway that alerted him.

The door had opened swiftly, and just as swiftly Carter had Wilhelmina in his hand.

He dove behind the desk.

The explosion in the office was small, as if contained under glass.

Carter leaped up. He didn't have a gas mask. He took a deep breath and raced through orange and gray smoke toward the door, wondering whether it had been the hefty beer maid or the disgruntled boss who'd told the wrong person about his presence.

Almost instantly he felt the fumes on his skin. He was in trouble. It was the kind of gas that didn't have to be breathed.

He crashed through the door, Wilhelmina raised.

Rough hands grabbed him.

He struggled to turn, fight, shoot, escape.

Too late. His skin had absorbed the gas. He collapsed in the hands of his kidnappers.

—from PURSUIT OF THE EAGLE
A New Nick Carter Spy Thriller
From Charter in April

☐ 74965-8	**SAN JUAN INFERNO**	$2.50
☐ 71539-7	**RETREAT FOR DEATH**	$2.50
☐ 79073-9	**THE STRONTIUM CODE**	$2.50
☐ 79077-1	**THE SUICIDE SEAT**	$2.25
☐ 82726-8	**TURKISH BLOODBATH**	$2.25
☐ 09157-1	**CARIBBEAN COUP**	$2.50
☐ 14220-6	**DEATH ISLAND**	$2.50
☐ 95935-0	**ZERO-HOUR STRIKE FORCE**	$2.50
☐ 03223-0	**ASSIGNMENT: RIO**	$2.50
☐ 13918-3	**DAY OF THE MAHDI**	$2.50
☐ 14222-2	**DEATH HAND PLAY**	$2.50
☐ 29782-X	**THE GOLDEN BULL**	$2.50
☐ 45520-4	**THE KREMLIN KILL**	$2.50
☐ 52276-9	**THE MAYAN CONNECTION**	$2.50
☐ 10561-0	**CIRCLE OF SCORPIONS**	$2.50
☐ 06861-8	**THE BLUE ICE AFFAIR**	$2.50

Prices may be slightly higher in Canada.

Available at your local bookstore or return this form to:

CHARTER BOOKS
Book Mailing Service
P.O. Box 690, Rockville Centre, NY 11571

Please send me the titles checked above. I enclose _____ Include 75¢ for postage and handling if one book is ordered; 25¢ per book for two or more not to exceed $1.75. California, Illinois, New York and Tennessee residents please add sales tax.

NAME _____

ADDRESS _____

CITY _____ STATE/ZIP _____

(allow six weeks for delivery.)   A8

THE ETERNAL MERCENARY
By Barry Sadler